WHO'S GETTING MARRIED?

PORT SIMMS
BOOK ONE

ANN ROTH

OLIVERHEBERBOOKS

Cover art by Dar Albert at Wicked Smart Designs

Published by Oliver-Heber Books

0 9 8 7 6 5 4 3 2 1

❀ Created with Vellum

CHAPTER 1

Bad things happen in threes, and Violet, aka Vi Preston, was about to get hers. Not of the small variety, either, but real heart-stoppers, the kind that hits hard to the chest, turns the blood cold, and makes a person want to throw up.

The signs were there before dawn Friday morning, before the Port Simms, Washington, April sun peeked through the clouds and before the robins, Steller's jays, and song sparrows even thought about starting up with their welcome-to-another-day calls.

Vi and her black tom cat, Mr. T, the only male she'd kept in her life for more than a few weeks, liked to wake up gently. Which was why she'd programmed the workweek alarm to nudge her awake and start the day off right with a favorite U2 oldie, *It's a Beautiful Day.* Oddly, something went haywire and an ear-breaking squeal overriding the music blasted through the bedroom. Startled, she jerked up. Screeching a meow that just about out-boomed the noise, the tom cat darted under the bed.

Groaning and wondering what'd happened, she stabbed

the off button. The squealing stopped, thank you, God. No problem, she'd reload the song later. But the abrupt wake up had rattled her. Never mind, this was sure to be a banner day. Thanks in part to her leadership, DD Telecom was strong and thriving. With the outstanding performance review she was sure to get this morning and the promotion and subsequent raise that came with it, plus a nice quarterly bonus, life was good.

Now, if she could shake the sense of unease from that wakeup…

By nature anxious, she forced her mind elsewhere and thought about tonight and the surprise in store for Gran. After work, she had a dinner date with her at the 709 Retirement Community. The first meal invitation since Vi and her sister Rose had moved her in three weeks earlier. Rose couldn't make tonight, as she was visiting a luxury spa in Cancun for another week or so. She was the gorgeous sister, while Vi was average-looking with the most smarts.

The retirement home rules were clear: a trial period of six weeks was okay, expected even, because a person needed time to decide if they liked the place. After that, it was either buy or vacate the premises. Gran was halfway through the trial period. In that short time, she'd made friends and was already talking about staying. But she didn't have the money to cover a down payment on her unit.

Not counting Rose and their divorced parents, Gran was the only other member of the family. Years earlier, as a newish widow, her husband Chester having passed away, she'd moved into their childhood home when their father had left for Hawaii with his girlfriend, leaving their mom to hold down two jobs with little time to see them. Gran worked, too, but found time to love and take care of the girls. She'd been the one stable adult in Vi's life—no drama, no arguments or fighting. She meant everything to Vi, and she and Rose planned to help her buy that unit.

They had it all figured out. Rose's surgeon husband Peter had plenty of money. Granted, their thirteen-month marriage was a little rocky, partly because he spent so much time at the hospital or away at medical conferences. He softened Rose's feelings of neglect by financing her shopping sprees and travel, and she indulged herself with reckless abandon. Unfortunately, he wasn't willing to donate more than a fraction of what Gran needed to buy her unit at the 709. Vi was supposed to come up with the rest.

Every penny of the bonus was earmarked for the down payment on the apartment. Vi was going to spring the good news on Gran at dinner tonight.

While Mr. T cat-strolled toward the kitchen to either await breakfast or use the kitty litter box in the utility room off the townhouse's kitchen, Vi padded toward the bathroom and thought about the increased income from her raise and what it meant for Gran's future.

Normally, she listened to the morning news while showering and dressing. Today, she left her phone alone and thought about the performance review ahead. Between that, her raise, and Rose's monthly contribution, their grandma could easily manage the mortgage payments. "This will be an amazing day, so forget the abrupt wake up noise and be happy," she told herself, her words echoing in the shower stall.

Yet anxiety hovered like a flittering hummingbird throughout the shower and continued as she stood in front of the bathroom mirror and turned this way and that in her new spring dress, an outfit that screamed rising company star and an upcoming career move to a more profitable team. Once again firmly ignoring the nameless sense of unease, she calmed her wavy, flyaway dark-brown hair with taming conditioner. Her attempt at an everything's-fine smile failed, and her reflection frowned back at her.

She threw up her hands. "I don't have time for this." Lips compressed, she headed for the kitchen to feed the cat and make coffee and toast. The tom quickly devoured half the food—a dainty eater, he'd nibble the rest throughout the day —and stood at the door, wanting to go out. "You know that isn't safe," she said.

She'd barely sipped the coffee and hadn't even spread honey on her peanut butter toast when she realized the kitchen clock, which was synchronized with the atomic clock in Colorado, had slowed to a sloth's pace. The LED said seven thirty-three, when according to the cell phone it was actually eight-ten. Which gave her twenty minutes to get to the meeting on time. Shoot, should've replaced the battery.

Todd Melton, her boss and a senior vice president with the company, had scheduled the performance appraisal for eight-thirty, giving her ten minutes to make the twenty-minute drive. He was a stickler for punctuality, but then so was Vi. Except for this morning.

Bad thing number one, and the fault was hers alone. Who knew what the next two would be?

Muttering, she sloshed the coffee into a to-go cup, scooped the toast up in a paper towel, threw her purse strap over her shoulder and rushed out the door.

As she backed out of the driveway, she sent a text to Todd, letting him know she was stuck in traffic. On the drive, her cell signaled more than a few texts. Which was odd. Probably friends wishing her good luck today. She didn't want to listen to them now. After the appraisal.

At the red lights, and wouldn't you know she hit almost every one, she gobbled the toast. It was the last food she ate until dinner.

ACROSS TOWN, standing in his soon-to-be second BW Bikes store, Blake Wanamaker alternated between relief and stress. Relief that Daisy had ended their relationship last night. She was way more serious than he was and in too big a hurry to move ahead. Stress because she'd also resigned as the head of recruiting and hiring. Getting the store open and running by May first had been problem-riddled enough before she'd quit. Now it'd become a giant pain in the ass.

From the start, he'd known better than to hire a woman he was seeing to work for him. Dumb move on his part. How was he supposed to know she wanted to get married? He certainly hadn't led her on. No hot kisses or any kind of fooling around. Heck, they weren't even serious, and she knew it.

Now he needed a replacement for her, and fast. He hadn't had much luck with recruiting companies, but maybe he'd give it another try. Otherwise, he'd be stuck doing the job himself when his plate was already heaped way too high.

His cell phone chimed with a call. Grandpop, the one person in his life he could depend on. Short-tempered now and then, but steadfast and true. He didn't phone during work hours unless it was important. Bypassing the noisy workmen whipping the unfinished space into shape, he stepped outside into the coolish morning. "Hey, Grandpop. Everything okay?"

"Better than ever." Words Blake hadn't heard from his lips in years. While he wondered at that, Grandpop went on. "You're awful calm. What's wrong?"

The man knew him so well. Acting and sounding relaxed meant he was stressed, fallout from dealing with a high-strung mother. He glanced at the sky. The clouds couldn't decide whether to dump rain or skittle past and let the sun shine down, normal weather for an April day in the Pacific Northwest. "You know how it is opening a second location— you opened dozens."

"Only ten before I franchised. Trust me on this, each time is easier. You and I haven't talked in a while, and I sure as heck haven't seen you. Seems to me, you could do with a break. Come to dinner tonight. They're serving roast beef or lasagna, your choice."

It'd be good to see the man, and the 709 served decent food. Blake scrubbed a hand through his hair, which had gotten long due to lack of time for a trim, and blew out a breath. "Wish I could, but I have a lot to do, including recruiting and hiring staff."

"Surely not on a Friday night. I thought Maisy or Daisy, or whatever her name is, was in charge of that."

"She was, but we broke up last night, and she quit."

"Let me guess—she wanted to get married."

Yup. "She invited me out to eat last night and proposed. I turned her down."

"That was fast. I'm not surprised she fell for you. You have a way about you that women seem to like."

Love hadn't played into Daisy's proposal. Nope, she

wanted a man to take care of her and had chosen him. Or so she'd strongly hinted. Little gold digger.

"I only met her the one time when I stopped by the new store to take a look," Grandpop said. "She wasn't your type. But you're thirty now, and I could do with a grandbaby. I understand that after your engagement to Sammi fell through, you got scared about marriage. But that was several years ago, and you're over it, so lose the excuses and start looking. It's high time you settled down."

Unwanted advice Blake ignored, but he couldn't let his grandfather's words stand uncorrected. "The decision to call off the wedding was mutual," he reminded the man.

"Then what's holding you back, boy?"

"In case you haven't noticed, I'm kinda busy with the business." Plus, having had a front-row seat to what happened when things ended in a good marriage had made him wary. When his dad had died unexpectedly some twenty years ago, his mother had gone off the rails. In his view, she still was. She'd been engaged multiple times and had recently signed her second set of divorce papers in four years. Currently, she was in an ashram in India, trying to find herself.

No, thanks. "Whitney's pregnant with your first two grandchildren—twins," he reminded Grandpop.

"And I'm thrilled. Two is a good start, but it'd be damn nice if you added to the gene pool, too. I'm 78 years old and won't be around forever."

"Don't try to guilt me. You're healthier than anyone I know." Blake changed the subject. "So you think I have a type. Tell me, what would that be?"

"No idea. I haven't met her yet. I ordered the lasagna for

7

you. If you want the roast beef instead, I need to get the changed order in."

He expected Blake to follow through on the dinner invite, and barring emergencies Blake always had. He owed the man a great deal. After his father had died, Grandpop, Blake's maternal grandpa, had been a good role model for him and Whitney. He had a gruff side but was solidly behind them and loved them when their mother was wrapped too deeply in grief to pay much attention to them. He'd walked Whitney down the aisle on her wedding day and had also advised Blake on business issues and loaned him the seed money to open the first bike store. It'd be good to see him, and Blake really did need a break. "I'll stick with the lasagna."

"Excellent choice. I reserved a table for six o'clock and am playing bridge at seven-thirty. Don't be late."

CHAPTER 2

The second bad thing happened shortly after Vi stepped through the door of DD Telecom. There was no sign of the usual cluster of employees drinking coffee and chatting in the lobby before the company opened. Weird. Had she missed something? Frowning, she finally checked the messages on her phone.

An emergency all-employee meeting had been scheduled in the big conference room. That explained the multiple texts from this morning. The unease she'd felt earlier flooded back, and she hurried upstairs to the meeting room on the second floor. It was packed. Todd stood at the podium, his tie slightly askew and his blue button-down shirt strained across his middle-age belly. He raked a hand through his hair. Twice. Had to be bad news.

She found an empty seat next to Eric, a short-lived boyfriend from the IT section of the business until their amicable split almost a year earlier. Like all the guys she'd dated over the past several years, he was a nerd. In the worst sense.

The guy kept his shoes in a pile under his bed and left dirty dishes in the sink all day, both of which drove her nuts. What a slob. He also spent a great deal of time drinking and partying with friends, reminding her all too well of her parents before the divorce. She had no interest in wasting her time and didn't care if she never saw him again. But as they worked for the same company, she maintained a civil relationship with him. "What's happening?" she said in a low voice.

"Brace yourself. Alan Ragen has bankrupted us. He was forced out last night and the company filed for Chapter 11 bankruptcy."

The CEO had done *what*? Certain she'd misunderstood, she gawked at him. "I don't understand."

Eric was about to say more when Todd adjusted the microphone. "I'm sure you have questions. So do I. I didn't find out about this until late last night. Here's what I know. Alan got himself into a dicey financial situation. He needed cash and stole it from the corporate account. I have no idea how he did it or why the accounting team didn't catch on until a few days ago. All I know is, he's gone and the company is in financial straits. We'll be laying off half the staff, and—"

Reaction was swift and loud. Angry voices roiled through the air, momentarily silencing him before he continued. "I'm every bit as upset as you are. If you're laid off, you'll be summoned to HR today to discuss your severance package and meet with a job counselor."

This couldn't be happening! Vi had never been timid and wasn't now. She stood up. "What about our bonuses?" And her pay raise and promotion?

"That's a good question, Vi. I've been told there's barely enough money to cover payroll, let alone bonuses. That includes mine. The board of directors has chosen Tarleton Iglesias as our CEO. For those of you who don't know him, he's been with the company for six years and is highly regarded."

Vi barely heard anything after the word bonuses. She crossed the fingers of both hands. *Please, please don't lay me off.* An acrid taste, sharp with fear, made her wince. Her throat had dried up, and she reached into the smaller of the pockets in her purse for a breath mint. She gave Eric one, too, and he needed it. The mint helped with the bad taste, but not the panic flooding her stomach, the same unpleasant feeling that signaled the money woes she'd experienced throughout her childhood.

Besides helping Gran—if she didn't have the money to permanently stay at the 709, where would she go?—there were bills to pay. The mortgage, car payment, et cetera, including Mr. T's last vet bill for surgery to remove bladder stones, to name a few. Expenses her barely adequate savings account couldn't possibly cover. Should've put more money away. Too late now.

"What do we do next, sue?" someone asked over the noise.

"We could, but unless the company has a way to pay, I don't know that we'd get anything from it. Consulting an attorney can't hurt. In the meantime, I'll keep you informed."

* * *

BLAKE ARRIVED at the 709 a few minutes early. Several residents and guests sat chatting in the lobby, a comfortable carpeted space with pleasant watercolor paintings on the walls, a large fish tank filled with exotic fish, and padded armchairs grouped here and there. As required, he stopped at the front desk to sign in. Another person was in front of him, an attractive female he'd seen somewhere but couldn't place. Long legs, slender, hair twisted in a knot at the nape of her neck, she wore a dress that draped her hips and hinted at her round behind.

"Vi Preston," she told Charlotte, the fifty-something woman behind the desk, in a no-nonsense tone, like a businesswoman with no time to waste.

The unflappable Charlotte checked her in. As Vi turned to leave and glanced at him, she arched her brows as if surprised to find him there. Almost as if they knew each other when they didn't. "Oh," she said.

Whatever that meant. He noted the sudden flush on her face. Like his grandfather, he had that effect on women. He'd inherited his looks from the man. "Hi," he returned, flashing his friendliest smile. "Have we met?"

"No, but I saw you here the one time I visited. You were with your pregnant wife." She glanced around. "I don't see her today."

She'd noticed him? That explained the eyebrows. "Now I know where I saw you. You were with two other women, one around your age, the other a senior. I'm not married. That pregnant woman is my sister. She's expecting twins. I'm Blake Wanamaker. Nice to meet you, Vi Preston."

"How do you know my name?" Tiny lines that made her look suspicious appeared between those eyebrows.

"You didn't exactly whisper when you announced it to

Charlotte. Not that you were overly loud. You have a voice that carries."

For the most part, women seemed to like him. Not this one. She pursed her lips in a disapproving way and raised her chin a notch. Although he had a good five inches on her, she somehow looked down her nose at him.

"You have family here, too," he said in an effort to coax some warmth into her.

"And I don't want to keep her waiting."

She spun away before he could reply. Ah, well. Can't please everyone.

Blake stepped up to the desk and smiled. "It's good to see you, Charlotte."

Unlike Vi Preston, she returned the smile. "You too, Blake. Your grandfather mentioned you'd be here tonight."

Curious to find out more about Vi, even if she was ice cold, he said, "It's always interesting to meet new people here."

Charlotte glanced behind him at the line where other guests waited to check in. Better get going, as Grandpop was expecting him. "He's waiting for me now. Have a great weekend."

Eager to see the man, he forgot all about the less-than-pleasant encounter. As soon as he entered the dining room around the corner from the lobby, he spotted her again, her long legs swinging straight for Grandpop and a female about the same age with silver hair also seated at the table and in cozy conversation with him. Blake was taken aback, had assumed the dinner would be just the two of them. His grandfather hadn't mentioned other people at the table. And now Vi was joining them? What were the two seniors up to?

13

She wouldn't be happy to see him again. The prospect of enduring a meal with her didn't sit well with him, either, but it'd give him a chance to get on her good side if only to see if he could. Whatever the reason for this dinner, it was bound to be interesting.

CHAPTER 3

Bad thing number three for Vi: dinner at the 709 with Blake Wanamaker and his grandfather. Of all the things that could happen, this was almost as bad as what'd gone down at work today. At least she'd managed to keep her job. The only ray of light, if you could call it that.

But dinner with that man? Why, oh why? He was extraordinarily handsome if you didn't count the shaggy hair parted and styled like some movie star—not a good look—with piercing eyes that unnerved her. Like most good-looking men, his ego was the size of Mount Everest. Standing at the check-in area and attempting to charm her with a smile and friendly chit-chat was about as phony as a guy could get.

No, thank you. Surviving middle school and high school with boys who routinely made fun of her had hurt. Back then, she'd been saddled with a lot. Taking care of the house and her sister for as long as she could remember, even after Gran moved in—both she and her mom worked long hours—she'd stayed up late to do homework. The drudgery of her life had kept her from smiling much. She'd been dubbed ugly, humor-less, an egghead.

She'd survived. Then in her junior year of college—But she didn't want to think about that and pushed the past away. Before anyone at the table caught sight of her, she slipped into the women's bathroom to collect herself.

The room was empty. As she washed her hands, the past flooded into her mind after all. She'd met Devin on campus at the University of Washington. Not as a student—he worked on the grounds crew that tended the campus landscaping. He was cute and buff, and to her surprise, interested in her. No guy with his looks had ever pursued her. Flattered, she'd agreed to meet for coffee. Soon, they'd started seeing a lot of each other. There were things she hadn't liked about him—skipping work for no reason, evasive answers when he showed up late or canceled a date at the last minute—but she'd ignored all that. It hadn't taken long before she'd fallen hard for him.

Then he'd borrowed money from her, promising to pay her back but never seeming to have the funds. She caught him cheating with another girl and confronted him. She expected him to apologize and promise not to do it again, but he'd shrugged her off and headed for the door without a single word. She'd pleaded with him to stay and talk it through. Instead, he'd walked away.

Leaving her with a smaller bank balance, a broken heart and utter humiliation for begging him not to go. What a fool she'd been.

Never again.

At least she'd learned her lesson. As an average-looking woman, she preferred the company of less handsome males who knew they weren't God's gift to women. Not that she had much luck with them, either.

So no, she wasn't happy about the table for four tonight. But Gran was expecting her. She headed again for the dining room. Her plan had been to let her grandma know she wouldn't be able to help with the down payment. Impossible without her bonus and the promotion and raise. Without the raise, helping with the monthly payments at the 709 would be a struggle. Gran couldn't return to her former tiny one bedroom apartment, as it'd been rented to someone else.

The waiting list at other retirement homes was months long. Vi didn't have room in her townhouse. She tried to reach Rose that afternoon, but no luck. Her sister was likely basking in the attention and pampering at the spa. Vi texted her to call but hadn't heard back.

If Gran couldn't go to Rose and Peter's—which would bother Peter and Gran would hate—where else would she go? That was a big worry.

She approached the table with trepidation—what were the two males doing there? Gran and the man who she assumed was related to Blake sat next to each other, which forced her and Blake to do the same. He bore a striking resemblance to the older man. Same intense navy eyes, proud Roman nose, strong chin and wide mouth. Sitting beside him made her nervous. The entire setup did. What was happening?

"Hello there, young lady," the older man greeted her. "I'm Malcom Essex, Malcom to you. Addressing me as Mr. Essex makes me sound too old." Behind his gold-frame bifocals, his eyes twinkled.

He seemed nice, and Vi relaxed a little. "I'm Vi," she said, managing a slight smile.

"So I assumed. Have you and Blake met?"

"Briefly at the check-in desk," Blake answered. "We didn't know we'd be dining together." He widened his eyes at her, as if wondering how the evening would play out.

"That's right," she agreed, and caught herself finger checking the twist at her nape to ensure it was tidy. Making sure she looked as good as she could for him? Of course not. Sometimes it got loose and she didn't want that to happen at the dinner table. "I assumed it was just you and me tonight, Gran." Blake nodded that he'd guessed the same. "Exactly why are we eating together? There are several available tables here, so I know it's not a space issue."

Gran and Malcom exchanged looks that could mean anything, and Gran beamed at Vi. "Isn't my granddaughter beautiful? She's smart, too, and up for a promotion at her job."

As if she were trying to sell Vi to both men. Weird and embarrassing. Also untrue. She wasn't the beauty of the family. As for the promotion, the sooner she shared the bad news, the better.

While she attempted to ignore the false praise, Malcom spoke. "That's wonderful, Vi. Blake is a successful business-man. BW Bikes is doing so well, he's about to open his second store."

Blake looked as puzzled by the sales pitches as she was.

"It's nice that you and Malcom are friends, but why are we all at this table, and what's going on here?" Vi asked for the second time.

Gran opened her mouth to comment just as the meals arrived. As soon as the server, who looked to be in her twenties, left, Gran spoke, but not to answer the question. "Smells wonderful, doesn't it? Let's have dinner first and get to know each other a little. Then we'll talk."

"There's no reason why we can't talk while we eat," Blake said and dug into his food.

"I'm with him," Vi seconded. "By the way, this roast beef is delicious."

"So's the lasagna." Blake eyed her. "First time you've eaten here?"

"My sister Rose and I had lunch on the day we brought Gran to look around. She signed up for a unit and we celebrated with a meal. She's been here just three weeks." She glanced at her grandma. "This is the first time I've been invited to eat with her since. Just me tonight—Rose is in Cancun for two weeks."

"Nice. So you and Grandpop have known each other for three weeks, Mrs.—what should I call you?"

"Caroline is fine. And yes, we met that very day."

Malcom nodded. "Caroline's unit is on the sixth floor, the same as mine, only without the panoramic view of the Pacific Ocean and the islands scattered around."

"What I see from my living room window is pleasant enough," Gran said. "I look out over some of the gardens and the parking lot. I enjoy watching people coming and going in their cars. We met as we headed downstairs for the happy hour offered every evening before dinner. Those of us there gathered around a big table—like me, a fair number of people who live here enjoy socializing over a cocktail or mocktail and Chex mix. I consider many of them friends now. We had such a good time that Malcom invited me to join him and another couple for dinner. We've been dining together ever since and not always here. There are many good restaurants in this part of town."

"Some afternoons and evenings we play bridge," Malcom added. "Sometimes we see an afternoon or evening movie in the area. Although neither of us likes to drive at night. That's why I founded Falcon Ride Service years ago, way before Uber and Lyft."

"Yet another enterprise that made him even more successful," Blake pointed out.

Malcom nodded. "I sold it awhile back, but I'm a loyal customer." He winked. "And I never have to pay."

Gran nodded and smiled. "He's a shrewd one, all right. Don't forget our walks. And tennis. We've only played once, when the weather was nice. We're lucky to both be in decent shape."

"And I'm glad of it," Vi agreed. "Are these get-togethers usually the two of you?"

"Sometimes, but we're both sociable and often invite friends to come along. Or they invite us. Couples and singles. I'm very happy living here."

The two seniors shared a fond look. They hadn't known each other long, and reminded her of teenage kids certain they were in love, brief romances that faded almost as quickly as they developed. It wasn't at all like Gran to latch on to a man. She hadn't been romantically involved with anyone since Grandpa Chester had passed away some twenty-plus years earlier. Seeing her gaga over Malcom, who she barely knew, didn't sit well with Vi. She set her fork down.

From Blake's squinty-eyed study of the couple, he didn't approve, either. "You two have gotten cozy awful fast," he said.

Gran was in for disappointment when Vi told her that due

to finances, she wouldn't be able to live here much longer. Wanting to get that news off her chest, she cleared her throat. "I need to speak with you, Gran. Privately."

"But we haven't finished dinner, let alone had dessert. Tonight it's cherries jubilee or fudge cake. You don't want to miss that. Can we talk later?"

"I'd rather do it now."

"Go ahead, Caroline," Malcom said. "Blake and I will hold off finishing our food and wait for you here."

"Please, not until after dessert," Gran insisted. "I'd like to finish the meal first."

What was the big deal? At the pleading expression on her face, Vi relented. "All right, if that's what you want."

She tasted the dessert, which was good, but having lost her appetite, she mostly pushed it around the plate. Shortly after the server whisked the food away and delivered the after-dinner coffee, Gran and Malcom shared another look and a nod.

"We have something to tell you," he said.

Unable to imagine what it could be, Vi leaned toward them while Blake muttered something unintelligible.

"We've decided to get married," Malcom announced.

Vi gaped at her grandmother, and Blake choked on his coffee.

"WHAT THE HELL?" Blake said none too softly as he dipped his napkin in his water glass and dabbed at the coffee splotch on his shirt. Was the man out of his mind? "Let me get this straight—you've known each other three short weeks and you want to get married? You can't do that."

"We can and will. We don't need your approval." Stubborn man that he was, Grandpop narrow-eyed him and folded his arms across his chest.

"No, no, just no," Vi said, backing up Blake.

Caroline's tightened jaw let him know she was stubborn, too. "This is a good thing," she told Vi. "I've been widowed since your Gramps died. It's been a lonely existence. Still, I never expected to fall in love again. Now I have. Once you come to terms with our decision, I hope you'll approve."

"With or without it, we'll marry." Grandpop uncrossed his arms and clasped Caroline's hand. "You're the love of my life."

Bull. "Grandma was the love of your life," Blake corrected.

"My current life. Grandma passed three years ago. She'd want me to find love again, and I have." He lifted Caroline's hand to his lips.

Blake shared a look with Vi that was every bit as anti the half-brained idea. "This is so unlike you, Grandpop. Have you seen a doctor lately? Do you think you had a stroke?"

"Don't insult me, boy," he chastised in a voice Blake hadn't heard since his teen years. "I'm seventy-eight years old, and I know what I want."

"You and I need to talk. Now," Blake argued in no uncertain terms.

"Fine, fine." Grandpop heaved a sigh and rose. "I'll see you at bridge later, Caroline."

"Us, too," Vi said. She and her grandma headed off somewhere.

Blake and his grandpa went straight to the library, a large room that resembled a booklover's den with shelves of books.

By day it was busy, but in the evening few people used the room. For now, they had it to themselves. They sat down in comfortable armchairs made for settling in with a good book. Blake went straight to the point. "I questioned you about seeing a doctor because what you're doing isn't like you. I'm concerned."

"This is exactly like me, so put your worries away. I know what I want, and I feel great about my decision. Haven't been this happy in a long time."

His bright eyes twinkled, confirming the words. He appeared to be relaxed and supremely confident about his decision. Blake felt the opposite. He didn't care for this new side of his grandfather and didn't trust it, not when things were moving so fast. No one in his right mind decided to get married after knowing someone for a mere three weeks. "That's nice. You're aware that Washington is a community property state."

"Of course. I've lived here all my life." Grandpop squinted at him. "You're afraid she'll inherit my money instead of you and your sister. Is that what this is about? Well, rest easy. Robertson Wolfe has been my attorney for forty years. When I die, you and your sister will make out very nicely."

"So you've said." Before Caroline, but things had changed. Then again, Blake and his sister were doing well without relying on the man. Yes, he'd financed the first bike shop, but Blake had repaid what he'd borrowed and was doing fine on his own now. "It's your money, not ours. Still, I think you should slow down and take your time. If you and Caroline are truly meant for each other, waiting awhile won't hurt. If after time passes and you're sure, that's great. But if you get married and your feelings change, things can get ugly." Caroline seemed nice enough, but his grandpa barely knew her. Blake didn't want her going after his fortune.

"I'm not naïve, Blake. Robertson's drawing up a prenup now."

Grandpop had thought of everything, which was reassuring. "I'm sure Mom would like to know about this. Have you been in touch with her?"

"You and I both know that ashram doesn't take kindly to contacts from outsiders. It's part of the deal there. But if she gets hold of me, which we both know is doubtful, I'll tell her. Why, have you heard from her?"

Blake shook his head. He'd always been an afterthought in her life and likely always would be.

"I thought you'd be happy for me," Grandpop said. "But it's obvious you're not."

"Can you blame me? You spring this on me with no warning, and three weeks is too soon to be sure. That's why I'm questioning your judgment."

"Well, stop. I love this woman, and she loves me. We want to be together, live in the same unit and share a bed. We can't do that unless we're married."

"You don't have to get married to sleep together."

Grandpop smirked. "We've been doing exactly that."

The thought of them having sex... Blake didn't want to think about that and managed to hide his reaction. "Can't you continue the way you are?"

"Not if we want to live together. There's a rule here about that. No cohabiting."

Blake frowned. "Why is that?"

"No idea. That's just how it is here. As soon as we're

married, we'll move to a bigger place. I have my eye on something on the top floor that'd be perfect. Caroline likes it, too."

He talked about the unit they wanted to share, but Blake didn't pay much attention. He was thinking about the marriage rule at the 709. It made sense and kept things from getting sticky when one person got sick or worse. Which, face it, was bound to happen as people aged, even if they were in good condition now. "Sounds nice, but what's the rush, Grandpop?"

"We have to move quickly, before Caroline does something she'll regret."

Blake had no idea what that was about. "I'm not following."

"Her daughters have offered to help her with the down payment on her unit, but she's decided not to take their money. She's too proud."

Blake didn't like the sound of that. "Are you saying she doesn't have the money in hand?"

"She will, once she cashes out her life insurance policy. According to her, it's worth a fair amount. She's looking into that now."

Although they were the only two in the library, Grandpop leaned in and lowered his voice. "She doesn't know this yet and won't like it, but I don't plan on letting her use her money to help pay for the unit."

"What do you mean, you won't let her?"

"Just what I said. Paying for the whole thing myself will be my wedding gift to her."

"That'll cost a bundle."

"So? I'll get a partial refund on my current place." Grandpop shrugged. "Anyway, I have more money than I'll ever need."

And the story kept getting worse. "And Caroline's okay with that."

"Did you not listen to what I said? She has no idea I'm footing the entire bill. She'll be okay with it."

Blake didn't like the sound of that, but wasn't surprised. For all he knew, Caroline had planned the whole thing shortly after the two of them had met. In the few years since Grandmom had died, more than a few women had plotted to marry him and get their hands on his money. He'd seen through them and steered clear. Until now. "Gold diggers come in all ages."

"Caroline is no gold digger." Grandpop's face reddened and he stood up. "This conversation is over."

CHAPTER 4

"We have a lot to talk about," Vi told Gran as soon as they entered her unit. It was small but comfortable, with a little kitchenette and table off the living room and a decent-size bedroom and bath. Through the large picture window in the living room, pretty white lights lit the peekaboo view of the garden for security purposes and nighttime walks. Easier to see were the parking lot lights and cars parked there.

Gran didn't say anything until Vi closed the drapes and they sat down on the sofa. Then, "You're not happy about Malcom and me, are you?"

"To tell you the truth, I'm in shock. He seems nice enough, but you've only known him a few weeks. It's too fast, Gran. If I were doing this, you'd say the same thing."

Her grandma made a *pfft* sound. "How could you know anything about it? You've been in love exactly once, way back in college. For all of what, six weeks?"

Over the years, Vi had grown used to her outspokenness. Even so, the words hit hard. She wanted to trust enough to love someone again. But between Devin and the scars from middle and high school, she was jaded. "Excuse me for being skeptical, but you've fallen in love even faster." For all Vi knew, Malcolm wanted a helpmate to take care of him as he grew older. She didn't want her grandma used like that. "As for me, the right man hasn't come along yet, but when he does, I'm sure it'll happen."

"Maybe if you didn't find fault with every man you've dated, you'd have better luck."

Nothing new there. Gran thought she was too picky. "What's wrong with being careful? I refuse to settle for anyone who falls short."

"I think that's wise, but your standards are so high, finding anyone who rises to them is close to impossible."

Vi raised her chin. "That's not true."

"Oh, no? Let me refresh your memory with a few recent examples. You didn't like the way Casey ate with his mouth open. Larry had a good job. If you'd given him half a chance, he might've worked out, but you didn't like the sound of his laugh, so you ended that. You did the right thing with Eric, though. I didn't like him."

At least they agreed on Eric. Vi sighed. "Let me set you straight about the other two. Casey had no table manners at all. He was an utter slob with terrible B.O. I ended things with Larry because his shoes were gross and he wouldn't get them repaired or buy a new pair. Plus, he expected me to see films he enjoyed and eat where he wanted to go. He refused to see any of the movies I suggested, and he always made excuses to eat at his favorite places even when he knew I didn't like them. He paid more attention to his ferret, Ralph, than me. That thing never liked me, and it smelled. Tried to bite me, too. Larry thought it was funny.

"All clear signals that I was at the bottom rung of what he cared about." He was selfish in bed, too, and didn't wash his sheets often. "Why would I put up with anyone like that?" The way she had Devin. "But this conversation isn't about me."

"You're right. At my age, moving fast is okay. I'm seventy-seven years old, and Malcom is seventy-eight. He's a good man and treats me well. We love each other. Can't you and Blake be happy for us?"

"So love each other. There's no need to get married. You live on the same floor." Time to deliver the bad news. Vi cleared her throat. "At least for now."

"Exactly."

What was she getting at? "You lost me."

"Aren't you talking about moving?" Gran asked.

"Yes, but how did you know?"

"Because—why don't you go first, Vi."

"All right. I got some bad news at work today. Our CEO embezzled money. Lots of it. The board fired him last night and has filed for bankruptcy."

Gran's mouth hung open. "No."

"It's true."

"That's terrible. Is DD Telecom closing their doors? Does that mean I have to switch to a different phone service, and what about my TV and internet?"

That was all she cared about? "The company won't close, but they've tightened the purse strings. Things should be okay. Tarleton Iglesias, a man with smarts and integrity, fingers crossed, is going to run the company now. He was hired the year before I was and seems like a good fit. But to save money, half the workforce was laid off." Most of them good people with great skills. "I wasn't one of them, thank goodness, but I didn't get my bonus or a raise."

"That's a shame. I'm glad you're still employed."

"You and me both. But, Gran, without the bonus I won't be able to contribute anything toward your down payment here. I doubt Rose will be able to help much, either. I'm afraid you'll have to leave the 709."

"You're right, Peter would never allow Rose to use his money on me. It doesn't matter—I've already decided not to accept any money from either of you girls."

"But we offered our help and you agreed."

"No worries—I've decided to cash in my life insurance policy. I made up my mind about that almost as soon as I moved in. It means you and Rose won't inherit anything from me, and I'm sorry about that. But I'd feel terrible making you girls shell out your hard-earned money on me when I have the funds I need."

"After all you did for us when we were growing up, we want to help out. Or did until this bankruptcy. We don't care about that insurance policy, we care about you. Your social security and pension only stretch so far. Wherever you end up staying, we can still help with the rent."

"No, thank you. This is good news. Be happy I can take care of myself. Malcom and I are looking for a bigger unit and think we've found it, but I can't pay my share without cashing in the policy."

So much to take in. Vi's head was spinning. "Have you contacted the insurance company?"

"I left a message with my insurance agent this afternoon."

"What if there's a problem or the policy isn't worth what you think it is?"

"I'm sure there's enough, but if there's a problem, Malcom will know what to do."

Vi was horrified. "You can't put him in charge of that, Gran. It's really none of his business. Besides, he may not know a thing about insurance."

"If I know him, he'll want to help. He's very smart about business things. Otherwise, he wouldn't have founded AM Auto Parts and franchised it so successfully."

Everyone had heard of that company. Vi was impressed. "He's the man behind that?" Was Blake part of the business, too?

Gran nodded. "You don't get that successful without hard work and a whole lot of brain power." She sighed. "I love a smart man."

"Gramps was smart, too," Vi said to remind her about her dead husband. He'd died when she was ten, and she could barely remember him. Four years later, when her parents had divorced, a big relief because they were always fighting, Gran had moved in to help take care of her and Rose.

"He wasn't stupid, that's for sure. After all, he married me." Gran smiled. "Chester was a good man, and so is Malcom." She glanced at the digital clock on the wall. "It's late and I'm sure you're tired after the long work week. I have a bridge game to get to." She stood. "It'll be interesting to find out what Malcom and Blake discussed. Goodnight, Vi."

She'd never been shy of announcing when she wanted guests to leave. Fine with Vi. She wanted to phone Rose and commiserate over the bombshell Gran and Malcom had dropped on her tonight. She kissed her grandmother's proffered cheek and opened the door. "Have fun at bridge. I'll talk to you again soon."

* * *

IN THE LOBBY after the unsettling conversation with his grandpa, Blake headed toward the front desk to sign himself out. Vi was already there, doing the same. This might be a good time to strategize next steps and all that. Tonight, as he had so much on his plate besides the love and marriage thing they'd sprung on him.

"Hey," he said. "Was your conversation as aggravating as mine?"

"I'm shaking my head. This entire thing is ridiculous, especially wanting to get married after knowing each other three weeks."

"Tell me about it. We should find a quiet place to talk. Are you in a hurry to get home?"

"Not really."

"If we hang around here when our family are playing bridge or sleeping, management might not like it. Let's go somewhere."

She glanced upward as if she needed to think about the idea, and the corners of her lips turned downward. Finally, with a look that was either dislike or contempt, she nodded. "You're probably right. Where are you thinking?"

Stung, he asked, "Do you have a problem with me?"

"Why would you think that?"

"The expression on your face when you look at me." She frowned again, and he told her. "Like I'm the last person you want to go anywhere with."

Her face got red, signaling she was embarrassed. "Sorry about that. I don't mind looking at you at all. You have a—" She blushed redder still and cleared her throat. "I'm so rattled right now, it's hard to think about anything else."

He wanted to know what she'd started to say but wasn't about to go there. They had more important things to discuss. "Do you know the Come On In?"

"The bar? I've eaten there a time or two and like the food. But it's Friday night and sure to be crowded and noisy."

"Good point. What part of town are you in?"

"The east side. You?"

"West. Pick a place near where you live and we'll meet there."

"Well..." She cocked her head to one side and chewed on her bottom lip, which for some reason he found cute. "How about the Pancake Hut? They're usually quiet in the evening."

"And the food is great. See you there."

On the drive toward the restaurant, Blake thought about the situation that'd been thrown at him and Vi. Talk about a punch to the gut.

She was right about the Pancake Hut—there were at most a handful of customers and one tired-looking waitress to take care of everyone. They sat down at a table with a laminated top.

"Believe it or not, I could use a waffle about now," Vi said as she pulled a pair of menus out of their slot beside the napkin holder and handed him one. "With strawberry sauce and whipped cream. I didn't eat much today, and lost my appetite at dinner."

"You and me both. My mouth is already watering for an egg and cheese pancake sandwich."

For some reason, she laughed. A nice sound and her whole face lit up. The transformation wowed him. Without the wary expression, she was one gorgeous female. "What's so funny?" he asked, smiling.

"The eager look on your face when you talked about food. I could almost picture you as a little boy."

Maybe in the days when his father was still alive. "I'm not only eager, I'm ravenous." He signaled the waitress over.

After she took their orders, Vi picked up the conversation where they'd left off. "I was stressed before I walked into the 709. My day was taxing enough without this."

"Something at work?" he wondered.

She nodded. "I'm a sales manager at DD Telecom. Last night, without anyone but the board knowing what was happening, they filed for bankruptcy and voted out Alan Ragen, the CEO. His replacement seems like a good choice, and I'm sure everything will work out."

She was solemn and earnest and attractive, and strands of her tightly bound hair kept fluttering around her face no matter how often she smoothed them down. Was she involved with anyone, and why did he care? Just last night, he and Daisy had split up. Anyway, this was no time to think about that.

"Oh, man, I hadn't heard." He'd been too immersed in getting his second store up and ready. "What happened?"

"I don't know much except that Ragen is responsible for bankrupting the company. Apparently, he embezzled a ton of money. My boss delivered the news at a hastily called meeting this morning. They also laid off half the employees."

Blake winced. "Sorry you got laid off."

"I was spared from that, but they let go of some of the

teammates I manage. And I didn't get my first quarter bonus or the promotion I was slated for."

"That sucks."

"And not only because it came as a shock. I was counting on that money to help Gran with the down payment at the 709. I knew nothing about Malcom or this so-called love thing till they announced it. At least I found what bad thing number three was—is."

"Because bad things always come in threes." His mother used to bemoan the same thing, and he deliberately ignored it. "You don't really believe that, do you?"

"I definitely do. First the bad news at work, second—" She broke off and shook her head. "Never mind about that. I'm curious, if you're running AM Auto Parts now, how do you have time to open a new bike store?"

Why she'd cut herself off, he'd never know. Now that she'd lost the ability to help Caroline out, both her question and the gold digger possibility made sense. He shook his head. "I've had nothing to do with the auto parts business. Grandpop sold the company and transferred his partnership in the franchises about seven years ago. Even before that, I didn't have anything to do with it."

"Why not?"

"Overseeing all those franchises and the daily stress of running a big company? Not for me. I was only twenty-three but smart enough to recognize I wasn't ready for that kind of responsibility."

"That's young to be so insightful about yourself. So you're thirty now—the same age as me. And you own BW Bikes."

"That I do." He puffed up with pride.

"I was in there once, to rent a bike for a few hours with a guy I was seeing at the time. It has a good feel to it."

"Always good to hear. What happened to the guy?"

"We were all wrong for each other. Story of my life." She looked horrified at saying that and covered her mouth with her hand. It was obvious she didn't want to talk about that.

He added to his story. "Like Malcom said, I'm getting ready to open a second store on the opposite side of town from the first one. It's a great location, about a mile north of where Henry Simms Highway leads into town."

"Isn't that where the paper mill used to be and was closed due to environmental pollution issues and lack of funds to pay for the cleanup?"

"That's the place. The mill is long gone and all sixty acres of land and the fresh-water lake are clean again."

"I read about that, but haven't been out there."

"You wouldn't recognize it. The land has been divided into a nature preserve and a development with restaurants, new homes, businesses, schools, churches and synagogues."

"Smart of you to locate the new store there. Have you put up a big sign letting tourists know where to rent bikes?"

"A 'coming soon' sign is up. Do you ride often?"

"I used to, mostly to run errands before I was old enough to drive."

"When I was a kid, I cycled all over, too, with friends or alone. That feeling of pure freedom… You never forget it."

"I never had much time to ride for the fun of it."

Her childhood sounded rough. His hadn't been a picnic, either. "Maybe your parents can talk some sense into your grandma."

Vi snorted. "I wouldn't hold my breath. My father lives on

the Big Island in Hawaii with—let's call her a free spirit—he left my mother for. They've been there sixteen years now and are into surfing and partying. I have no idea how they survive, but I think she has money. We only talk on holidays and birthdays. My mother lives in Houston and does hair and nails when she's not out partying."

"They're both that way, huh?"

"Like they're barely old enough to drink, only in their fifties." Her expression was pure disgust. "You should know that Gran is the most stubborn person I know. Once she makes up her mind... Well, unless a decision causes harm to someone, she rarely changes it."

"Grandpop is the same way. Even he calls himself a stubborn cuss. That doesn't bode well for their marriage."

"What about your parents? Maybe they can talk sense into Malcom, even if he is bullheaded."

"Wouldn't that be nice. It won't happen. My dad passed away after a freak accident when I was ten. Almost did my mother in." Since then, she'd all but forgotten Blake and Whitney. "Dad's parents, Grandpop and Grandmom, stepped up and helped out." If they hadn't, Blake and his sister would've been in a world of hurt.

"I'm so sorry. What happened to your mom?"

"Five years later, she finally came alive again. She'd been a secretary at Port Simms Elementary and got tired of the job, so Grandpop hired her to run his front office. She was happy enough there and finally started dating. A whole string of boyfriends, until she met someone she wanted to marry.

"They relocated to Sedona. The marriage failed and she moved on to someone else. A few months ago, she went through her second divorce. As you can imagine, she's pretty messed up. Right now, she's at an ashram in India, trying to find herself." He snorted in doubt. "I texted her, but she took a vow of silence and isn't supposed to speak or communicate with the world. When she's allowed to get in touch, I'll update her. She'll want to know about Grandpop and will worry about her share of the inheritance."

"I don't blame her. My Gran shouldn't get a penny of that money."

Knowing Vi sided with him was a relief. "We're agreed on that. Hey, what was with them bragging about us?"

"I was so embarrassed. It's the kind of thing people do about their kids and grandkids. But in front of us and to someone we just met? Gran has never done that. Not to my face."

"Grandpop has, but not like tonight. Go figure, right?"

"With no parents to help us with this situation, we're on our own here. What are we going to do?"

At the moment, Blake had no idea. "Anything and every-thing we can to stop this wedding."

"Or at least delay it till they come to their senses. They both need time to be sure this is what they want." Vi yawned, covering her mouth with her hand. "We need a game plan, but right now I'm too tired to think about that."

"I'm pretty wiped out myself. I have a lot on my plate right now. Opening the second store and other things, like finding someone to interview future employees and put them through an orientation."

"There are people who do that sort of thing, you know."

"I hired one, but she quit last night. She wanted—I don't need to get into that. You wouldn't know of anyone familiar with conducting interviews or training new employees to get them up to speed, would you? Maybe one of the people laid off at your company?"

Vi shook her head. "Not that I can think of, but if someone comes to mind I'll let you know. Why don't you hire a recruitment firm to do the work for you? My company uses Ace Recruitment, and most of the time it works out."

"I probably will, but I'd still want the candidate to go through a second interview with me and make sure they have decent people skills and the smarts to hire employees and lead them through orientation. Once I find that person, my life will be a whole lot easier." He shrugged. "A real pain, but that's the way I operate."

"Apparently, it didn't work with the person you hired for the job."

May as well tell her. "I made the mistake of hiring the woman I'm seeing—make that *was* seeing. We split up last night, and she quit."

Her disapproving, pursed lips showed what she thought of that. "Sounds messy. I'm sorry you broke up."

"Hey, it's not your problem. I knew I shouldn't hire her, but she really wanted the job. She left a pile of unopened employment applications instead of doing the work I hired her for, so good riddance. At least I have some people to interview. It's all good. I'll contact that recruiter company first thing tomorrow—if they're open Saturdays. I don't want to wait long for us to get together again. What about Sunday afternoon? You free? I'll text the deets."

"You'd better believe I'll be there. Time is one thing we don't have."

CHAPTER 5

S aturday morning, Vi heard from Rose. "Got your text," she said by way of hello. "What in the world is going on?"

"I'll get to that in a minute. Tell me about the spa."

"It's fabulous, the best I've been to. Tasty, healthy food, friendly people, great places to walk and work out. The shopping in the area is also good. I'm already planning to come back next year. Hey, why not join me? It's not as pricey as you'd think."

Wouldn't that be nice?. "As much as I'd like to say yes, we'll have to wait and see."

"Come on, Vi, you never pamper yourself. A me-time vacation is just what you need. I shouldn't say this, but I don't miss Peter at all," Rose added.

Their relationship seemed to wax hot and cold, but Rose had never said anything like this. "That doesn't sound good."

"We're okay. I think we needed a break from each other. I have a massage scheduled in a little while, so please get to the point. What's so important that talking can't wait till I get back?"

"You're gone for another week, and so much has happened. I'll make it quick, I promise." Skipping most of the details, Vi started with the DD Telecom bankruptcy and the postponement of her bonus and raise—if she was lucky enough to get either one. "You know what that means. I can't help Gran with the down payment."

"That's terrible about DD Telecom. You must be so disappointed. Poor Gran will be booted out of a place she likes. I know from when we looked for a senior retirement home for her before, we kept running into long waiting lists. It was so frustrating. Where will she live?"

"If I had room, she could bunk with me. Your house has a spare bedroom with its own bath. I was hoping she could stay there until we found her something else, but—"

"Living with her would be hard. I doubt Peter would go for that."

"Gran wouldn't want it, either. Anyway, it doesn't matter anymore. You won't believe what's going on with her."

"Don't tell me she's sick?"

Lovesick, maybe. "Not in the way you think." Vi filled her in.

When she finished, Rose's disbelieving huff came through loud and clear. "That can't be true. Gran wouldn't fall in love and certainly wouldn't think about getting married, especially so quickly."

"You'd think. You should see the way she and Malcom make googly eyes at each other. It's enough to ruin your appetite. Blake is just as upset about it."

"Who?"

"Malcom's grandson." Vi explained that the older man was wealthy and moved on to Gran's decision to cash in her life insurance policy to help finance their move into a bigger unit.

"They want to live together at their age? That's crazy. If this Malcom person has all that money, why can't he pay for the whole thing?"

"You know Gran. She's adamant about paying part of the cost."

"She was willing to take your bonus money for the down payment."

"Only because we're family and we guilted her into it. She's changed her mind and decided to make the down payment for the unit by cashing in her insurance policy."

"Boy, I sure wouldn't, especially if someone else offered to pay. I'd be fine with it. Even if I wanted to use my own funds, Peter wouldn't let me. If I suggested anything like that, he'd have a fit. He likes taking care of me financially."

Vi suspected her sister put up with him for that very reason. And a good thing, as her part-time job at a boutique didn't pay much. She lived a lush life, even if Peter kept a tight rein on his money. "Yeah, well, you're not as headstrong as Gran."

"That's for sure. I had to sign a prenup before Peter and I got married. Does Malcom want the same?"

"That's a good question. Blake might know. I'll see what I can find out from him."

"Is there a reason they want to get married so fast?" Rose asked.

"Blake asked Malcom about that in private, at the same time Gran and I had our little chat. Both say they're in love and don't see any reason to wait. So odd for Gran, and according to Blake not Malcom's normal behavior, either. I'm guessing the real reason for the rush is that Gran's supposed to make the down payment on her unit sometime in the next three weeks. It'd be crazy to use her life insurance proceeds for the unit she's not planning to stay in and then hassle with getting the money refunded so she and Malcom could live together."

"That's understandable. What's stopping them from cohabiting now, which I don't even want to think about, and getting married later? Or not at all."

"Because it's against the rules at the 709. A couple have to be married."

"In the twenty-first century? I don't remember anything about that coming up when we first visited the place."

"Why would it have? Gran's been single since Grandpa died, and none of us ever imagined she'd meet a man and fall in love. When you think about it, the rule makes sense. If an unmarried couple move in together and one of them passes on, a definite possibility when you're in your late seventies, who owns the unit? I'm no lawyer, but that's my take."

"That makes sense. Let's hope Gran lives for a long time yet."

"Amen. Anyway, Blake and I met up after we left the 709 to discuss the situation. We're both in shock. We need a strategy of some kind to stop them or at least slow them down and—"

"Hold it right there. Don't say another word till you tell me about Blake."

"But you have a massage to get to."

"Yes, darn it. When I'm home again, I want to hear about him."

Vi doubted there'd be much to say. If all went well, by then he'd be out of her life.

* * *

ON THE OTHER side of town that same morning, Blake contacted Ace Recruitment. Unfortunately, the company was closed on weekends. He called Ross, a buddy and biking partner who'd worked at the original BW Bikes store several years earlier. Ross knew how the business worked and could do the preliminary interviews. "It'll be a short-term gig," Blake said.

"You got me at a good time. I'm looking for a new job."

"You didn't mention that when we went out riding a couple weekends ago."

"Because I hadn't given my notice yet. If this hiring thing works out and you're happy with me, maybe I'll stay. I need a steady job."

"That'd be great. I could use a hand getting this new place ready to go and then running things when I'm at the other store." Blake wasn't going to hold his breath, as Ross's employment track record proved otherwise, but for now he'd do.

He set up a meeting at the new store for that afternoon. Then he texted Vi with the time and place to meet the following day. Good thing she'd agreed to get together on Sunday.

An hour later, Ross showed up right when he'd said he would, a positive sign. He and Blake were roughly the same height, six feet, both of them lean and mean, thanks to the cycling they enjoyed.

Blake showed him around the shop. "As you can see, there's a lot more to do here before it's ready, but the construction team tells me they'll finish up in the next week and a half."

"When is the opening?"

"May first, a good three weeks from now."

"That's soon. Cool, though—cycling and tourist seasons will be in full gear then. This is a nice space and a great location. You're gonna be busy. Tell me about this work you want me to do."

Blake explained about interviewing prospective employees and, if Ross stuck around, training them. "Heading up HR," he added.

"I thought Daisy was in charge of that."

"She was, but we broke up Thursday night. Then she quit."

"Say what? This happens a lot with you. I mean break ups."

"Yeah, I know. She invited me out to dinner after work that night, at least that was the plan. Then in the parking lot, she proposed."

"No way. That's a new one."

"Caught me by surprise. She wanted a man to take care of her and chose me. She thought I was a fat cat." He wasn't hurting, was more than comfortable, but not wealthy by any stretch.

"That's harsh. You guys were together for what, two months?"

"Barely six weeks." He shook his head. "Can you believe that?

"I'd run the opposite direction so fast."

"I didn't need to. She fed me a line about love, and asked if I loved her."

"Let me guess. You said you like her but don't love her."

"Of course. Who falls in love after six weeks?" Except Grandpop and Caroline. Blake made a face.

"So she broke up with you."

"Saved me from doing it. She quit the job, too."

"I'd be so relieved."

"I am. Anyway, this morning I found a dozen or so applications she hadn't done anything with—another reason I don't mind that she quit."

"Wow. There are times when it's good to be a serial monogamist."

"Is that what I am? I don't stay with anyone long enough to fit that description."

"What do you call it?"

"Playing the field and enjoying myself." Safer that way. "You're not exactly a long-term relationship guy yourself."

"Not now, but I'm thinking about it. I'll be thirty in two years and want to get married and have a family."

"Where's that coming from?"

Ross shrugged. "I met this girl, Britt, at Bain's when I needed a new tent for a hiking and camping trip this summer. We've been going out a lot. I really like her. You're already thirty. Don't you want to settle down?"

"Depends."

"On what?"

Blake hadn't figured that out yet and didn't want to discuss it. He handed over a folder of the job applications. "Take a look at these and see what you think. Some might work out, others not. You'll want to contact each applicant and set up meetings. Are you comfortable with interviewing people?"

"I can do that. When do you want the interviews to happen?"

"If possible, Monday morning. It'll be noisy here, with the construction crew working, but you can meet at Hastings for coffee. There's one a few miles south. If anyone seems interested and wants to see this place, feel free to bring them by. I'll be here."

"Sounds good." They talked about money and Ross agreed to show up the following Monday at nine. They shook on it. "I appreciate this," Ross said and left.

That done, Blake texted Vi. *Can you meet me here at the new store midmorning tomorrow to brainstorm?* He gave her the address. The contractor didn't work weekends, and he wanted to show her around.

She replied right away. *I'd like to see your new store. Around 10? Funny, a few minutes ago an idea popped into my head about the marriage situation. It'll take me about 20 minutes to get there.*

So far, he'd drawn a blank and was eager to hear what she'd come up with. Whatever it was, it'd be a good place to start. Surely between the two of them, they'd come up with something to keep the grandparents from doing what they might regret.

CHAPTER 6

Saturday night, Vi was supposed to meet her bestie, Carmie, at the Majestic, a dine-in movie theater, to see a new film. But there was so much to talk about, they changed their get-together to The Come on In, a blue-collar diner Blake had mentioned the other night, some five miles south of the 709.

The cafe was crowded, but Carmie had arrived a few minutes earlier and put their name on the wait list. Meanwhile, they huddled on a bench outside, bundled up because in early April nights tended to be chilly.

"I didn't have time for lunch today, and I'm really hungry," Carmie said. "You wouldn't believe how busy we were." She worked for Port Simms Apartment Rentals. "It's like this every spring. What's so important that you traded a movie and dinner night to talk?"

Vi was about to tell her everything when the hostess paged them that their table was ready. "Let's order first, then talk," she said when they were seated. "I know what I want—a burger with cheese, onion rings, and a glass of shiraz. It goes well with burgers."

"A great pairing," Carmie agreed. Then laughed. "We sound so sophisticated."

Vi grinned. "Well, of course."

As soon as the waitress left with their orders, she updated her friend about DD Telecom.

"Unbelievable." Carmie shook her head. "Are you planning to stay there?"

Vi had never considered leaving. "Why wouldn't I?"

"If it were me, I'd look for another place to work, just in case."

"I don't have anything to worry about. Our company is too big to fail."

"Until it does. After what happened to my mom, I'm paranoid." Carmie's mother had been laid off when the hardware chain where she worked had declared bankruptcy and was swallowed up by a bigger company that'd promptly laid off most of the workforce.

"DD laid off half the staff, but they kept me. They value my skills, and I'm sure I'll be okay. I have so much more to tell you."

"What could be bigger than that?"

"Just wait." Vi shared what she'd told Rose.

Carmie's jaw dropped. "Your grandma is engaged? I'm so jealous." She'd been expecting her boyfriend Chris to propose for a while.

The food arrived and the conversation continued. "The engagement isn't good news," Vi said. "But this yummy food helps."

"So good. I want to know about Blake."

She sounded a lot like Rose. What was with the fixation on him? Vi tried to change the subject. "Don't worry about Chris. He's bound to propose eventually."

"Fingers crossed. Now, about Blake…"

So much for changing the topic. "As I said, he's Malcom's grandson." Also super smart and delicious to look at. A strong, straight nose, navy eyes and long eyelashes she envied, a sensual mouth—no wonder he exuded confidence. But, ugh, that hair was a shaggy mess. She had to repress the urge to shove it off his forehead. At the same time, she envied how nice and thick it was. The opposite of her flyaway hair, which wasn't likely to hold its style.

His judgment wasn't so good, either. Bad enough he'd hired his girlfriend to take an important job. Not a smart move businesswise. On top of that, he'd broken up with her and she'd quit—no surprise there. Other than needing someone to replace her on the job, he didn't seem to care about her at all. More proof that good-looking men who knew their effect on women used it to suit their needs. Sleep with them, move on. She'd been fooled once. Never again.

It was a good thing she wasn't attracted to him. He wasn't attracted to her, either. Men like him didn't give women like her a second look, a simple truth that had been seared into her. The only reason they were in contact was to strategize how to stop their grandparents from making a mistake they'd all regret.

"You haven't known him long, yet you seem awfully familiar with him," Carmie persisted.

She wouldn't let up until Vi told her more. "When your grandparents make a snap decision like ours did, you become allies fast."

"Are you sure that's all he is?"

Her friend's knowing look bothered her. "We just met, Carmie. Anyway, he's not my type." She wasn't about to mention tomorrow's meeting. No sense stirring her friend up even more.

"Why, is he good-looking?"

Vi frowned. "What kind of question is that? But, yes, he falls into that category." Understatement of the year when looks-wise, the man ranked way up there. Except for the hair.

"I only ask because you always shy away from cute guys."

For good reason. "There's nothing wrong with being realistic. It saves me a lot of disappointment." Although, truth be told, most of the guys she dated disappointed her. The important thing was, she didn't get hurt.

"You're still letting Devin mess with your life, and I wish you'd stop. He doesn't deserve to be a speck of dirt under your shoe."

Carmie and Rose were the only people who knew about how she'd foolishly overlooked Devin's shortcomings and begged him to stay. Ugh.

"I happen to know that he's been divorced three times," her friend went on. "He barely graduated from high school and works for a roofing company as a day laborer. Right here in Port Simms."

Vi gaped at her. "He lives here and you never told me?"

"To tell you the truth, I never thought much about it. I didn't think it was important."

"You're my bestie, Carmie. You should've said something. What if I'd run into him?"

"He's been here a while and you haven't yet. And, yes, I

guess I should've let you know. He upset you so much, and I worried you'd go through that again."

"I get it, but I don't need you to protect me."

"You're right. I'm sorry."

"I forgive you. When did he come to Port Simms?"

"I believe he moved when he married his second or third wife."

"How do you know all that?"

"Social media. Look it up. Not all cute guys are creeps."

"I know that." Vi didn't see the point of developing feelings for a man who could have his pick of women far more attractive than she was. Why take that chance? "Can we stop talking about this now and order dessert?" She signaled their server.

They ordered, and Carmie went on. "One more thing— you're a beautiful woman, and don't forget it."

Hardly. "Maybe you need an eye exam. I'm smart and good at what I do, but I'm average looking, and that's okay. We both know Rose is the beauty in my family."

"You're every bit as pretty. Where's your self-confidence? Ooh, here comes dessert. I love hot raspberry cobbler with ice cream."

There, the conversation ended. As they finished the meal and parted ways, Vi shook her head. How had her tell-all turned into a pep talk instead?

* * *

VI WAS STRANGELY EXCITED to see Blake's new bike store, not to mention the man himself. Only because they needed to hatch a plan to stop the grandparents from making a huge mistake, and two heads are often better. Or so she assured herself several times. She liked Blake a little too much, a man she barely knew and handsome to boot. Clearly, she was out of her mind.

She reached the bike shop determined to ignore her unwanted feelings. A blue van bearing the BW Bikes logo along with the phone and website link was parked in front of a brand-new two-story building.

Apparently the building was still under construction. A prominent Coming Soon sign listed a coffee house, a food market and the bike shop.

The door was unlocked. She knocked to announce herself, then let herself in. Blake headed toward her. A black BW Bikes tee hugged his chest, which was broader than she'd realized, and emphasized his flat belly. Faded jeans that fit like they were made for him hinted at powerful legs. He greeted her with a friendly smile and a warm look in his eyes. Either he knew his effect on her or he found her attractive.

As if. Yet, want to or not, she felt all fluttery, like a high school girl with a crush. Refusing to stare at him one more second, she shifted her gaze to the store-in-process. The drywall was up but not painted. Windows, dusty from construction debris, added light to the room. The floor was concrete. "This is a great space, and a wonderful place to open your new store. Are you going to leave the cement floor as is?"

Blake shook his head. "I found a rubber flooring similar to what's in the first store. It's easier on the legs and feet."

"I hadn't thought of that. Do you know where you're going to put everything?"

He gestured at an unfinished counter. "Payment and order desk there. Bikes in the other room, merch on the wall over there. My office is in the back. Ace Recruitment is closed weekends and I'm in a hurry. I hired a former employee who used to work at the first store. He's become a friend and cycling buddy and knows the ropes."

"That's great. Do I smell coffee?"

He nodded. "I stopped at Hastings on my way here and picked up coffee and doughnuts."

Did he have to be so nice? "No way. How did you know I was craving both?"

His lips quirked. "Wild guess. After all, it's midmorning on a Sunday." He nodded at a pair of stack chairs with a little wood table between them. "Have a seat and help yourself," he said and set the coffee and the bag of assorted doughnuts on the table.

Vi filled both mugs and chose a doughnut. "Sometimes I meet my bestie, Carmie, at Hastings," she said as she dug in. "The coffee and doughnuts are excellent. I wonder if the cafe in this building will have treats as tasty."

"I'm counting on it." Cupping his mug in his big hands, he settled back and stretched out his legs.

She caught herself glancing at a certain part of his lap. She didn't think he noticed, hoped not. Her face went hot, and she cleared her throat. "Have you heard from Malcom?"

He shook his head. "What about you? Anything from Caroline?"

"No, and I'm not sure I want to talk to her until we have a game plan in mind."

"I'm on board with that. What's this idea of yours?"

"It's not well thought out, but as soon as it popped into my mind I liked it. Gran talked about contacting her life insurance company and cashing in her policy. My plan is to do my best to talk her into leaving it alone for now. Here's my reasoning. Finding a decent senior retirement home these days is impossible, but what if we find her an apartment where she can stay until she and Malcom get to know each other better and decide for sure whether they want to get married?"

Blake tapped his finger on his lips. "That's not a bad idea. Where did she live before?"

"In an apartment. She was tired of living by herself and ready to try living in a place filled with seniors."

"Grandpop felt the same way. She likes it there, right? She probably won't want to go back to apartment living even for a little while. Not if she's as stubborn as you say."

Vi blew out a breath. "It's a long shot, I know, but still worth a try. What've you come up with?"

"Nothing yet, except I keep thinking about the stubborn streak both our grandparents seem to have."

He wrinkled his brow in thought, not unlike his grandpa, and she had to ask. "Are you as stubborn as Malcom?"

After a moment, he answered. "I'd say I'm more tenacious than stubborn. What about you? Are you like Caroline?"

"I don't give up easily, and I have my own opinion about things. Does that qualify as stubborn, and what's the difference between it and tenacity?"

"Finally a question I can answer. Tenacious is determination to get what you want, going after it, and making needed adjustments along the way till you get it. Like when I searched for the right location for this space. I found out about this building and contacted the builder. His terms weren't what I wanted, and he didn't like my offer, so we negotiated until we reached an agreement. Stubborn is refusing to change your mind, period. Sound like anyone we know?"

"Certainly does. Where did you learn the difference?"

He gave a modest shrug. "I picked it up in business school. Same one Grandpop graduated from."

In that respect, not unlike Malcom. "Where did you go to college?"

"The University of Washington both for my undergraduate degree and MBA."

"One of the top ten best MBA programs in the country. I'm impressed. I also graduated from the UW, but I never saw you."

"With around fifty thousand students at the Seattle campus, that makes sense. What did you study?"

"Psychology." She'd worked her way through college to pay her way and was proud of that.

"Tell me you're not going to analyze me."

His wary expression made her smile. "I wouldn't know how."

"That's a relief. There's a lot of crap in there." He pointed at his head.

She wanted him to say more, but they were here to figure out how to slow the grandparents down. Stroking her chin like the long ago analysts in white coats she'd seen in old movies, she teased in a really bad accent of a German analyst, "You sound like a very interesting case. Tell me more."

His laughter bubbled through the store. "We should get back to brainstorming."

"Before I forget, my sister had to sign a prenup before she married Peter. Does Malcom expect Caroline to do the same?"

"That was one of the first questions I asked him. His lawyer is drawing it up as we speak."

"At least he isn't so blindsided by his so-called love to overlook that. Do you think Gran knows about it?"

"That's a good question." Blake squinted her way and seemed to be lost in thought. "If she doesn't know and he springs it on her, would she be willing to sign it? If not—"

"Maybe they'll both take a step back. I don't know her feelings about that, except she wasn't happy when Rose signed hers. If she doesn't like the idea, it'd be a good time to suggest she rent an apartment for a while."

"We need to find out ASAP. I'll be busy most of next week. Why not invite ourselves to dinner tonight. Unless you have plans."

On a Sunday evening? Vi's social calendar wasn't exactly hopping. She'd planned to order takeout and stream a movie, but liked Blake's idea. "Good plan. At the moment, slowing them down is at the top of my list."

"I'll call Grandpop right now on speaker phone." As he dialed, he signaled for Vi to be silent.

Malcom answered, sounding surprised. "Hello, Blake. Is there a reason why you're calling?"

"Yeah. I want to have dinner with you tonight, if there's room at your table."

"The dining room is closed Sundays. You know that."

Blake raised his eyebrows at Vi. "I'd forgotten. Where are you planning to eat tonight?"

"The Sea Captain's Café. Caroline and I have been several times."

Her mouth watering—the restaurant served fresh-caught fish that was excellent—Vi licked her lips.

Blake nodded his agreement. "Why don't Vi and I join you? We'll carpool. What time should I pick you up?"

"Listen to you two harp at us to rethink what we've already decided to do? No."

Well, shoot. There went that idea. Vi frowned, but Blake held up his finger signaling her to wait. He spoke in a calm voice. "Dinner ended abruptly the other night. It'll be a way for the four of us to get to know each other better."

A pause, then, "All right," Malcom said, sounding less-than convinced. "But one word about us changing our minds and we'll walk out. Picking us up is out of your way. It doesn't get dark till around seven-thirty. We'll drive ourselves. We like to go early and get a table before the place gets crowded. Meet us there at five." Without another word, he disconnected.

Vi was flabbergasted. "Did he just hang up on you?"

"That's his way of ending a phone call."

"But you're his grandson."

"He is who he is." Blake grinned. "And we're all set."

They high-fived each other, a brief contact of palms. No big deal, yet her body hummed. Probably because it'd been a while since a man had touched her in any way. Pathetic. Appalled at herself, she shifted in her chair. "I don't know if we're all set or not. You heard his warning."

"We'll work that out on the drive there."

"Five o'clock is early for dinner. I haven't eaten there in a long time and don't know what to wear. What do you suggest?"

His gaze roved over her, from her tie-dye sweatshirt and well-worn jeans to her loose ponytail, making her feel acutely self-conscious. "What you're wearing now is fine."

Did his eyes have to fill with the warmth she'd noted earlier? Her cheeks burned, but she knew better. Every straight male gave a woman that look, regardless of whether or not she appealed to him. They were wired that way. "These are my grungy clothes. I can't wear them to dinner."

"Up to you. I'll pick you up at your place." He handed her his phone. "Pull up your contact info. I'll do the same."

They held their phones close together and shared the info. She put her jacket on to leave. At the door, she paused. "We still need to figure out a subtle way to bring up the subject of the prenup so they don't feel ambushed. It'd be nice to figure that out in advance."

"Like I said, we'll come up with something on the drive to the restaurant. If not, we'll play it by ear."

"I don't do well without a plan."

"I'll pick you up at four-thirty," he said, effectively waving her concern away.

CHAPTER 7

T hanks to light traffic, Blake arrived early at the multi-unit complex where Vi lived. It was a nice area made up of newer townhouses. With spring in the air and the days growing longer, people were outside gardening in their small yards and visiting with each other or walking their dogs.

He passed a playground where kids played on the jungle gym and swings or shot hoops around a basketball court. Parking near Vi's place proved impossible. He soon found the guest parking area and pulled into a slot. Minutes later, he knocked at her door.

She answered, her eyes wide with surprise. "I was planning to come out so you didn't need to park, but you're early. Come in."

"There wasn't much traffic." Her dress highlighted her slender body. Tights and ankle boots showed off her nice legs. Damn, she looked good, good enough to kiss. As if. Theirs was a relationship borne out of a shared goal to stop their grandparents from making a big mistake.

That hadn't stopped him from wondering what she tasted

like. It'd been on his mind since this morning. There were times when he was a real jerk. He stifled his smirk.

"Is there something wrong with my clothes?" she said.

Hadn't realized he was staring at her. "I like that outfit," he answered, careful to mask his attraction with a casual tone.

She brushed off the compliment with a shrug, as if she didn't believe him. "These are work clothes." She nodded at his long-sleeve tee and pants. "I'm not the only one who changed."

"Felt like I should." He glanced around the main floor. "This is nice. From what I've seen so far, the whole complex is."

"I enjoy living here. The neighbors are friendly. My house isn't big, but it's just right for me. One of the few one-bedrooms here."

"And two stories."

"The bedroom is upstairs and there's a tiny second room I use as a home office. The rest is what you see."

Kitchen with eating counter and a small living room, all spotless. A large black cat strutted in the direction of the kitchen as if he owned the place.

"Who're you?" he asked, crouching down to greet the animal.

"That's Mr. T, come to check you out."

"Do I pass muster?" Blake asked him, running his hand down the shiny black fur. The cat began to purr, and he grinned. "I'll take that as a yes."

"Let me grab a jacket, then we'll go. Behave yourself, Mr. T. I don't see the truck," she said with a slight frown as they reached the visitors lot.

"I drove my car instead." He gestured at his red Lexus sedan.

"Cushy," she murmured.

"I like it."

"It wasn't in the parking lot this morning. The truck was the only vehicle I saw."

"I use that for business, this morning to bring in the stack chairs and little table so we'd have a place to sit. Ruby is for pleasure." The word flowed from his throat in a husky voice he hadn't intended. Maybe she hadn't noticed.

She glanced down, but not before he noted the sudden color in her cheeks. She'd noticed, all right. What was his problem? Best put the brakes on his attraction to her. Now.

"Ruby?" she asked.

"First time I've named a car. For some reason the name popped into my head. It fits. I bought her used after the bike shop's one-year anniversary." After months of pouring everything he had into succeeding. "I netted more than I anticipated and figured I deserved a reward."

"Must've been a very good year for you."

"Demand for bikes, whether to buy or rent, is huge. I bought Ruby from a customer's great aunt who'd given up driving. She'd owned it four years and had driven it only fifteen thousand miles."

Finally, a smile. "Lucky you. When I was promoted to sales manager a few years ago, I rewarded myself by buying this place. Dinner tonight won't be for pleasure."

"Believe me, I know. I keep forgetting to mention that Grandpop is planning to pay for the whole new unit himself as a surprise wedding gift to Caroline."

"She won't like that. She's too proud to take his money."

"It'll be interesting to find out what happens. Don't say anything to her."

She didn't appear to hear him. Too antsy. "You're nervous, huh?" he asked.

"I've been trying to hide that. What gave me away?"

"Your compressed lips and the way you keep fussing with your hair. By the way, that ponytail suits you." He liked it way better than her tight hairdo the other night.

"I wear it this way when I'm not at work. While we're at the restaurant, I'll try harder to pretend I'm calm. Without a plan, you should be nervous, too. We'll steer our way toward what we want to achieve tonight. If we do that, we might have a chance of reaching our goal. Otherwise, if we bring up the prenup point blank without easing into it, we risk them shutting down and leaving. We both heard Malcom's threat to do that, and I don't doubt he will. Tell me you've come up with something and help me relax."

"We have a goal. I don't think we can plan how we'll get there. It doesn't work that way and depends on the conversation." Now she was fidgeting with the sleeve of her dress. "Why does that stress you out so much?"

"I grew up in total chaos, and organizing my life as much as possible makes me feel more in control."

That explained the spotless townhouse. "Tell me about the chaos," he said, curious about her childhood.

"I already shared things about my parents. You really don't want to know more. We should spend our time strategizing."

"I'm genuinely interested. We have time—it'll take us a good twenty minutes to get to the restaurant. I know your parents are divorced and they both like to party. What else?"

"Now who's playing therapist?" she teased, then blew out

a sigh. "All right, since you asked... I don't remember my parents ever not fighting. Even when they went out together they were at each other's throats. It's a wonder they ever conceived Rose and me. They both worked, of course, and didn't have the time or energy to do much around the house. Rose is five years younger, and I pretty much took care of her. Meals, packing our lunchboxes, dinner... It was a lot."

Blake shook his head at that. "Sounds to me like you raised her. You carried a heavy burden on those young shoulders."

"I really did. Gran and Gramps helped when they could, but they worked, too. I was glad when my parents split up. Things got a lot quieter at our house. Then, when I was fourteen, Gramps passed away. Mom was juggling two full time jobs to pay the rent, buy groceries, and party when she could. Which wasn't as often as before, as she was dead on her feet.

"Gran needed a place to live and Mom needed help, so she moved in to take care of us. She did her best, took over some of the cooking and helped with the laundry, but being a waitress, she also worked long hours. For as long as I can remember, I was in charge of the house. I learned at an early age that making a schedule and a plan helped me feel in control. Now, aren't you sorry you asked?"

"Not at all." He felt for her. Before his father had died, his life had been great. "Your childhood sounds truly chaotic and you had way too much responsibility. That sucks. But there are times when having a plan doesn't work. Like tonight. As I said, we have a goal, and that's enough."

"But if we have a plan to reach that goal, we're less likely to fail. We can't be sloppy about this, Blake. It's too important."

"I hear that, but there's no way to predict what Malcom

and Caroline will say or how they'll act. The only thing to do is wing it."

"You may be good at that kind of thing, but I'm not. Tonight is really important. Too important not to have a plan. How can you be so calm?"

"This is the way I am when I'm stressed."

She gaped at him. "I'm jealous. What's your secret? How do you do it?"

"I don't know. Somehow I figured out that in times of stress, keeping my cool helps me think clearly. Sure beats driving myself nuts. Plus, it helps lower the anxiety levels of people around me."

"Not mine. I can't help how I'm wired. Give me an example how playing it by ear works for you."

"Think about dinner at the 709 the other night. We didn't have a plan then. We had no idea what was coming."

"Oh, I had a plan."

"How could you possibly? They sprung their marriage idea on us."

"My plan involved Gran and no one else. I'd tell her what'd happened at work and offer her an alternative to being out on the street."

"Moving into the extra room upstairs."

"That space is too small, plus there's no bathroom up there. I can't imagine her waking up in the night and having to come down the stairs to use the toilet. She's still steady on her feet, but what if she fell? My sister has a place with enough room, but her husband wouldn't like having Gran as a guest. Gran wouldn't like it, either, so it'd be a place to stay in the short-term. That was my plan."

"Then when Malcom and I were sitting with her at the same table, your plan went out the window. Yet you survived."

She exhaled a grudging breath. "True, but I was very uncomfortable. And I did follow my plan, just not at dinner. I told Gran when we talked later."

"That was an uncomfortable evening for all of us. Tonight will be different because we know what they want and what we want."

"Yes, but how do we lead them to agree to what we want?"

"You're a sales manager. Surely you know how to move the conversation toward a sale."

"With an internet or cable plan, yes, but using some of those techniques on my grandma... I'd feel dirty."

"You shouldn't. We're talking about a serious issue that has to be addressed and taken care of, no holds barred," he said.

"Until they walk out."

"There is that." She chewed on her lower lip, then clamped it between her teeth. Not having a plan for the evening was really doing a number on her. "If you bite your lip any harder, you'll hurt yourself," he warned. She needed to loosen up or tonight would be off to a bad start. But how to calm her down?

As he signaled to turn into the restaurant parking lot, he figured out exactly what she needed.

By the time Blake turned into The Sea Captain's parking lot, Vi was so nervous she felt sick.

"Hey," he said and reached for her icy hand. His fingers were warm and the reassuring squeeze comforting. "You're freezing cold. Why didn't you turn up the heat? Never mind. Listen, no matter what happens tonight, no one will die from it."

The instant he released her, she missed his grasp. "No, but the consequences could be—"

"Survivable," he cut in. "Ease up on yourself, okay? I can help with that."

Desperate to relax, she glanced at him. The steady strength she saw on his face soothed her nerves a fraction. "How?"

"Would you mind if I massaged your neck and shoulders?"

Rose swore by massages, but Vi had never had one. She wasn't sure what to make of the offer. "I hardly know you."

"Don't tell me you're afraid of me. I'm not a big, bad wolf, I swear."

"I know that. You can't exactly give me a massage in a public parking lot or inside the building. It won't be dark for hours yet, and people would see us."

He drove around to the far side of the restaurant where there were no other vehicles. "Now, we'll be out of sight."

Still undecided, she nibbled her lip. "Is it okay to park here?"

"I don't see any no parking signs." He drove past any windows and pulled to a stop.

Blake seemed like a decent guy, but for all she knew, he was a person who changed quickly and could be trouble.

"Hey, you need help and you need it now. Let me take your mind off your troubles. If what I'm doing hurts or scares you, say so and I'll stop. You have my word on that. No matter what, I'll finish by five."

He looked straight into her eyes with such earnestness, she gave in. "All right."

"Great. I can't do this in the front because of the center console. We should move to the back."

"This sounds like the old teenage excuse to make out."

"Does it?" His lips twitched. "The thought never crossed my mind."

She laughed at that and felt better. They climbed into the back, and she slid smoothly across the leather seat. "Now what?"

"Take your jacket off so I can do this right." She did, and he spoke again. "Now turn your back to me and let your head fall gently forward."

"Like this?" she asked, glancing at her lap.

"Perfect." His hands felt wonderful, so good she actually groaned. Instantly he stopped. "Does it hurt?"

"The opposite. Keep going."

"Your muscles are all knotted up," he said after a minute. "When was the last time you had a full body massage?"

"Never."

"Why not?"

She had no answer to that. "I don't know. I just haven't."

"You ought to get them periodically for health purposes. I do. You won't regret it."

All too soon, his watch beeped. "Time to stop."

Wishing he could keep going and grateful for what he'd done, she pivoted in the seat to sit beside him. Just the two of them in the car felt dangerously intimate. "I feel so much better," she said. "If you ever decided to give up the bike stores, you'd make a great masseur."

He chuckled. "I'll keep that in mind. Already, I see a change in you. You're much less tense. Repeat after me, 'whatever happens tonight, we'll all survive.'"

"Whatever happens tonight, we'll all survive. Maybe I *will* schedule a massage."

"Atta girl."

He lifted her wrist and kissed the sensitive underside—a first for her. Her heart thudded and her body reacted with longing. She let out a small sound of pleasure.

"Was I out of line? I didn't think about what I was doing, just did it."

"I don't mind at all." Overcome with gratitude and desire, she leaned up and kissed him on the mouth.

He pulled back and eyed her. "What's that for?"

"I guess I shouldn't have—"

He silenced her with a kiss of his own. She lost her train of thought and cupped the back of his head, urging him closer. His body was fit and hard, and he kissed like a dream, his lips tender and firm at the same time. And his hair, soft and thick... Shaggy wasn't so bad. She was really getting into it when he let go of her and pulled away.

"Why did you stop?" she asked, confused.

"Believe me, I didn't want to. We should go inside before they wonder where we are."

The dinner. She'd momentarily forgotten about that. She touched her hair. "Is it a mess?"

"A little. Do you have a mirror in your purse?"

She nodded. "It's in the passenger seat."

He reached between the front seats and retrieved it. One glance in the mirror—so many strands gone astray—and she pulled off the scrunchie, brushed her hair, and redid the ponytail. Much better. She glanced at him. "Yours could use smoothing as well."

She felt dazed, and while he set his hair to rights with his palms, tried to make sense of what they'd done. She'd never meant to kiss him, let alone get so involved in him. In them.

The whole thing was her fault. How could she have let this happen when she knew better?

Simple answer, he was irresistible. His skilled hands easing the painful knots from her neck and shoulders. The smell of him, a mixture of man and fresh air, his deep, soothing voice... All of it had seduced her. She hadn't meant to let things go this far, wasn't pleased with herself. Never mind, she'd put it behind her.

Blake was silent, no doubt regretting it as much as she did. "Okay now?" he asked.

She managed a nod. Neither of them spoke on the way to the restaurant entrance.

Once inside the door, he laid his hand on her upper arm as if reassuring her, then quickly let go. "We got this."

CHAPTER 8

Still reeling after kissing Vi—correction, after she'd kissed him and *then* he'd kissed her—Blake entered the restaurant at her side. She smelled faintly of something that reminded him of a field in the spring when new flowers perfumed the air. And that addictive mouth. Soft and generous, it'd begged for more than one kiss. He'd gladly obliged. She'd ignited a spark in him he hadn't felt in a long time, since the night he'd proposed to Sammi some four years ago. They'd mistaken passion for love. That and an uneasy feeling he'd never shared that he wasn't ready for marriage. Wouldn't let that happen again.

Delicious smells of freshly grilled fish, fried clams and other foods filled the air. At five o'clock, the place was almost full. Malcom had been right to score a table early, and he and Caroline had a good one with a view of Simms Bay out the window. Too bad the sunset was several hours from now. Watching the sun sink over the bay would've been spectacular.

"They're over there," he told Vi. Her faint nod was subdued

and calm, a welcome change from tension. On closer study, she looked as if she'd been soundly kissed. He hoped the grandparents didn't notice.

"Hey," he said, leaning in and talking close to her ear so she'd hear him over the chatter and clatter in the room. Despite the food aroma, he caught a whiff of her scent and wanted to pull her close for more. He quickly stifled the urge. "Put those kisses behind you and smile."

"What are you talking about?" She frowned at him. "I don't know where you get the idea that I'm still thinking about what happened. I'm not."

"Your dreamy expression says the opposite." That did the trick. The disgusted look she threw him obliterated all traces of the brief glimpse of passion she'd revealed in the back seat.

"Over-confident much? This is why I don't get involved with guys like you. There they are," she said, and strode ahead of him toward the table.

Guys like him? Smarting from that and aware of both Malcom and Caroline watching them, he forced a bland smile. As he approached the table a few steps behind Vi, Grandpop squinted a fraction, then murmured something close to Caroline's ear. With a curious look, she glanced from Blake to Vi.

"Hi, Gran, Malcom," Vi said loudly enough to be heard over the din. "Sorry we're a few minutes late."

"Your face is flushed," Caroline noted. "You're not coming down with something, are you?"

Paying no attention to Blake, Vi shook her head. They both knew kisses had put the blush on her cheeks. She took one of the two empty chairs, leaving the one beside her for him.

"Well, why are your cheeks so flushed?" her grandma persisted.

Blake didn't care for the scrutinizing looks the grandparents directed at them. "It's chilly out there," he said, "and we parked a bit away from the entrance."

Caroline seemed surprised. "That's odd. We had no trouble parking close to it."

"Didn't I tell you this place fills up quickly?" Grandpop said. "How are you two?"

"Fine, thank you." Vi picked up the menu. "I haven't eaten here in years. What do you recommend, Malcom?"

"Whatever suits you. It's all good. Caroline and I are in the mood for fish and chips. As we get further into fishing season, everything will be fresh caught."

Moments later, a college-age male server took their orders. Four cocktails, four salads, four fish and chips. They made small talk, Blake tiptoeing around the engagement and prenup. Vi shifted restlessly beside him, signaling her impatience to get to the point. "Relax," he reminded her under his breath.

She held off until the drinks arrived and the server delivered the meal. Then, shooting a quick glance at Blake, she spoke. "Are you still interested in the unit you mentioned the other night?"

Malcom nodded. "Yes, but it'll be another few weeks before we can move in." He took a healthy sip from his neat Scotch.

After a few minutes' silence, courtesy of digging into the meal, Vi wiped her hands on a napkin. "This is delicious, even better than I remembered. In the prenup agreement, who will own the unit if something, uh, changes?"

What had happened to subtle? Blake elbowed her. "Ouch," she said, none too softly. "I'm curious."

"We haven't discussed that—I haven't seen the agreement yet," Grandpop said. "My lawyer should deliver it sometime in the coming week."

Caroline tapped her finger to her lips. "I hadn't thought about a prenup."

She and Grandpop exchanged looks, and Blake caught his breath, waiting for a troubled expression that with any luck would drive a wedge between them.

But, no, she smiled. "I think it's a good idea, Malcom. That way you know I'm not marrying you for your money. I'm marrying you because I love you."

Looked as if the prenup wouldn't be a problem. Blake's hopes deflated like a leaky bike tire. He and Vi shared a now-what? look. The besotted seniors, busy with way too many brief kisses, didn't appear to notice. Blake was uncomfortable with the spectacle, and Vi muttered something about public affection.

"Stop it, you two," she said.

Make that ordered, not that it changed anything.

"What's wrong with a few light kisses to show our affection for each other?" Malcom asked.

Vi shared her opinion. "That kind of thing should be private."

Caroline's glare shocked her. "If you don't like it, look the other way."

"Come on you two," Blake said. "People are staring."

"Oh, all right," Caroline grumbled. "We'll make up for it later." She kissed Grandpop again.

Vi's groan of disgust let Blake know what she thought of

that. He was pretty grossed out himself. "This has been fun," he said, "but it's time I took you home, Vi."

The lovebirds didn't seem to notice or care.

As Blake was about to signal for the check, Vi held up her finger to hold on. "Wait'll Gran finds out about the down payment," she said, loudly enough that Caroline finally pulled away.

"What do you mean, Vi?" she said, frowning.

"Malcom has decided to foot the entire down payment on the bigger unit. He won't let you pay anything."

The frown deepened. "I don't understand. Is this true, Malcom?"

"It is." He gave Blake a dirty look. "Why did you tell Vi?"

"Why didn't you tell Caroline?" Blake shot back.

"Yes, why did you hide it from me?" Caroline's fists settled on her hips, a challenging pose impossible to ignore.

"Because it was supposed to be a surprise, my wedding gift to you." Grandpop's voice had risen to shout level.

Heads turned toward the table. "Well, I reject it," Caroline replied with equal heat. "I'm not a charity case, and it's important to me to pay my share. Which you know. We discussed splitting both the down payment and the monthly fees."

"You don't need to do that, and you *will* accept my gift."

"Don't you dare tell me what I will do," Caroline returned. "I won't."

No sign of affection now, not the way their eyes shot daggers at each other.

"Please, keep your voices down," Vi told them. "People are staring and it's uncomfortable."

Blake stood up. "Excuse me—I'll be right back," he said, but neither of the seniors seemed to have heard him or Vi.

He headed to the front of the room and quickly paid the bill. When he returned to the table, they were still going at it, although their voices weren't as loud. "Let's go," he told Vi, and they slipped out.

* * *

UPSET THAT HER comment had caused Gran and Malcom's very public shouting match, Vi shook her head as she and Blake neared the Lexus. "I feel bad about sneaking away like this, but they left us with no choice."

"We didn't sneak, we told them we were leaving. They were too wrapped up in their fight to either know or care. Pretty awful, huh??"

"I'm sure they'll figure it out, especially when the server tells them I paid the bill. What made you bring up Grandpop's plan to pay for the full down payment and not let Caroline chip in?"

"I didn't intend to, but it popped into my head and out of my mouth. Gran has always insisted on paying her own way. True, at first she agreed that I could use my bonus to make the down payment on her unit, but by the time I delivered the bad news about the company's bankruptcy she'd already changed her mind."

"Saying what you did was a smart move, Vi."

"Was it?"

She must've looked as appalled as she felt, because he said, "Don't feel bad—it's good they're fighting."

"Not to me. I hate fights." She wrapped her arms around her waist. "Reminds me of my parents."

"Our goal was to change things up between them so they'd

slow down and think more about what they really want. And we did, thanks to you."

"Only I didn't expect a yelling match." She'd never seen Gran so mad. "I figured they'd talk it through, maybe even argue, but not with such anger."

"Grandpop gets loud when he's rattled and always has. That's why I elbowed you when you brought up the prenup like it was no big deal."

"And I was right, it didn't faze either one of them. But someone had to get the conversation going again, and you didn't say a word. Now, if you'd warned me about his temper, I might not have been so straightforward."

"I probably should've. I kept quiet because I wanted to ease into the subject. I didn't want them to get mad and walk out. What a surprise when Caroline was fine with it."

"My comment about the down payment didn't work out so well. Instead of getting mad and leaving they got mad and stayed, and you and I walked out. The whole thing was mortifying." Vi shuddered. "I can't get over Gran getting that angry. I've never seen her like that."

"Never?"

"Not even when Rose or I did something she disapproved of."

"She probably knew you were traumatized from how your parents carried on in front of you. Maybe the fight will open their eyes to how little they really know about each other, and they'll rethink rushing into marriage."

"Let's hope."

"Don't look so miserable, Vi. You did great."

She had no answer to that, and he threw her a look. "'Thanks, Blake.' That's all you need to say."

"Thanks, Blake. If they had to fight, why didn't they wait till they were alone instead of going at each other in front of the entire restaurant?"

"On the plus side, they're not in la-la land anymore. Mission accomplished." A few minutes ticked by in silence, then he glanced at her with a teasing glint in his eyes. "Wanna go get dessert somewhere?"

Still unsettled and face it, super attracted to Blake, she hesitated. "I have to go to work tomorrow and should probably get home."

"Aw, come on. It's early yet, and you deserve it. We both do. Let's go to Melissa Ann's Bakery."

Her mouth watered. "They make the best treats in town. But I doubt they're open Sunday nights."

"They are, though. The schedule changed a few months ago. They're open until ten o'clock Friday and Saturday nights. Other nights, including Sunday, they close at eight." He glanced at the digital time displayed on the dashboard. "It's barely seven."

She couldn't turn that down. "Then take me there, please."

The warm grin that lit up his face took her mind off the unpleasant meal and caused all kinds of unwanted havoc inside her body. The kind that was dangerous. It was a good thing he was oblivious of her feelings. Otherwise, she'd be even more embarrassed than she'd been at the restaurant. Great kisser or not, he wasn't for her. Anyway, she'd be crazy to think he was interested in her like that.

"What's your day look like tomorrow?" he asked as they headed for the bakery. The sun was starting its slide toward the horizon.

Vi made a face. "To tell you the truth, I dread going in.

With so many people laid off, Friday was a zoo. I expect it'll be just as bad, only without Human Resources handing out layoff packages. At least that was handled competently and completed by the end of the day. Starting tomorrow morning, I expect we'll get a zillion phone calls from customers wanting to leave, and our day will be spent talking them into staying, etcetera. And me with a fraction of my team left."

"Sounds like the chaos you so enjoy."

"You have no idea. I'm so not looking forward to the mess ahead. But as a wise friend recently said, no matter what happens, I'll survive."

"You heard me." He grinned. "You learn fast. I'm glad we're friends." He glanced at her. "So what were those kisses about?"

Since he'd brought it up... "You helped me relax, and I was grateful. I reacted without thinking. You're the one who turned one little kiss into more. And FYI, I did *not* walk into the restaurant with a dreamy look on my face. Far from it."

"After those kisses, you sure did. You didn't stop me."

This was true. She gave him a dirty look. "It shouldn't have happened. You only broke up with your girlfriend a few days ago."

"I never said she was my girlfriend. We were dating, and yeah, I liked her, but not the way she liked me."

"What do you mean?"

"She proposed, a first for me. We'd been seeing each other about six weeks and never used the L word or anything close. That didn't seem to matter to her. She wanted a ring on her finger. When she asked me to marry her, I turned her down. Then and there, she resigned."

"Is she pregnant?"

"What kind of question is that? We never had sex. And

FYI, I always use protection. She saw me as comfortably well-off and wanted me to take care of her. Do I look like a fool?"

Vi wondered how many other women he'd dated and rejected. "Did she think she was your girlfriend?"

"Heck if I know. We never talked about it. Anything else you want to know?"

"I'm curious is all. If you don't want to answer my questions, I'll stop. I'll bet you date a lot of women."

"I do. But dating someone a few times is different from having a girlfriend."

Every comment he made reinforced what she already knew. He was a player. She wanted to smack herself in the head for kissing him. It wouldn't happen again.

"My turn." He glanced at her. "What's your boyfriend like?"

She was insulted. "Do you think I would've kissed you if I had a boyfriend? I split up with the last guy I dated ages ago. You didn't have to kiss me back."

"You're not easy to resist."

She so wanted to believe him, but… "Stop it, Blake. I'm too smart to fall for that. It was a mistake, and we're past it now. What's on the agenda tomorrow for store two?"

"The new floor gets installed, then the painting begins. Ross, the guy I mentioned this morning who used to work for me, has agreed to interview possible employees at the same Hastings where I got our coffee and doughnuts. I'll be checking in with him on and off. I plan to spend time at the first store, too."

"You're a busy man. Will you be able to manage both?"

"Not full-time. Danika is my second-in-command at the first location. She's great, but I like to keep an eye on things. It's one of the first pointers Grandpop taught me about running a business. I hope he and Caroline stopped yelling and started talking." He turned into the bakery lot.

Vi saw the crowd through the large front window. "I can't believe the people in there."

"This is why they're open seven nights a week. No problem—we'll get our stuff to go and find a place to eat it."

The line took forever, but at last they had a box of treats and coffees packed up.

By then, dusk had fallen. "Now to find somewhere to eat," he said.

"Or you can drop me back at my house. It's getting chilly outside, and I really don't want to sit in the dark."

"I wouldn't mind eating at your place."

Not quite what she had in mind. She was way too attracted to the man and wanted to get away from him, savor a cookie or two, and get to bed early. "I meant that you could—" drop me off on go on your way, she wanted to say, but his Bluetooth signaled a call from Malcom.

"Now that he's had a few hours to cool off, he's probably calling to apologize." Blake answered. "Hey, Grandpop."

"It's Caroline. We've been in a little accident and are on the way to the Emergency Room."

"What?" Blake frowned. "Why isn't Grandpop calling? Is he hurt?"

"A little banged up."

"A little?"

"What about you, Gran?" Vi asked, worried.

"I'm—oh, dear, I have to go."

"We'll meet you there," Blake said, but she'd already disconnected. "I wish she hadn't hung up like that." He signaled, checked for traffic and executed a U-turn.

CHAPTER 9

In a hurry to reach the ER which was a mile or so from the 709, Blake sped up the highway. Traffic was light, which was normal on an April evening before tourist season picked up.

"Slow down," Vi cautioned. "Otherwise, we could also end up as patients."

She had a point. He eased off the gas pedal. "As far as I know, Grandpop has never been in a car accident. He's a good driver, and it's barely dark out."

"It can't have been too serious. Otherwise, they'd be in an ambulance and on their way to the hospital."

"Caroline didn't say how they were getting to the ER, but if she's driving Grandpop's car, that can't be good." For the first time since his father had died some twenty years earlier, Blake was scared. "For all we know, they could end up at the hospital." The thought of his grandfather seriously injured was unbearable, and he swallowed hard as he braked for a red light. "Grandpop is like a father to me. If anything happens to him..." He clamped his jaw and gripped the wheel.

Vi laid her hand on his shoulder. He wasn't used to being comforted by anyone and wasn't a man who cried, but he was on the verge of losing his cool. "What are you doing?" he said in a voice that sounded gruff to his own ears. Better that than break down.

"The same thing you did for me—easing your worries." She took her hand away, and he was sorry he'd asked.

She didn't seem to take offense. "I feel the same way about Gran," she said softly. "She and Gramps were the only stable adults in my childhood. But sinking into the darkest place possible isn't helping. We don't know what the situation is. It seems to me if things were that serious, we would've heard from a medic instead of Gran."

"Why didn't Grandpop call instead?"

"I'm sure we'll get answers when we get there." She laced her fingers together in her lap.

The light turned green and he continued toward the ER. "We need info," he said. "It sucks that we're still a good fifteen minutes away."

"That's not so far, and you're making good time. I'll call Gran and put my cell in speaker mode." Caroline's phone rang and rang, but no answer. "Either she doesn't have it with her or she turned it off at dinner and forgot to turn it back on," Vi said. "I'll try Malcom instead."

"Forget that and contact the ER directly."

The voice message on that phone explained they'd answer in the order taken. "Must be a busy night," he grumbled.

"Someone will probably be on the line soon. We don't need to stew about what-ifs on the rest of the drive. Let's eat our cookies now."

He didn't have much appetite and only managed a bite or

two. Vi didn't eat, either. When he pulled into the parking lot at the ER some minutes later, her call was still on hold. She disconnected. The lot appeared to be full. "Be on the lookout for a parking spot," he advised.

"I see something the next row over." She swallowed. "I'm worried sick, Blake."

"You and me both." He pulled into the slot and they exited the car. Heart in his throat, he reached for her hand, and they headed for the door.

* * *

A DOZEN or so people sat in the ER waiting room, speaking in hushed voices. After what Gran had said about her condition, Vi had expected to see her and possibly Malcom seated and biding their time for their turn, but there was no sign of either of them. Seized with fear—was Gran more hurt than she'd let on and Malcom badly banged up?—she was glad for Blake's hand in hers.

They approached the front desk, where a harried woman took their names and asked them to be seated. "That won't work," Blake said. "We're relatives. We need to see them."

Magic words that allowed them to enter the hallway leading to the exam rooms. Wearing the masks handed out at the desk, standard protocol in the waiting room, they approached the nurse's station. "We're looking for Caroline Newberger and Malcom I'm, Debra," Blake said, his eyes on the name tag pinned on her shirt. "They're our grand-parents."

"But not married," Vi clarified.

Debra clicked the keyboard on the computer in front of

her. "Let me check their room numbers, Mr. and Mrs.—is it Essex or Newberger?"

"We're not married, either," Vi quickly explained.

"Definitely not," Blake added.

Debra looked appalled at herself. "I'm sorry, I thought—"

Blake flashed a quick smile, no doubt to put her at ease. "No problem. Where can we find them?"

As soon as they had the room numbers, they started down the hallway. Vi leaned slightly toward him, felt his warmth, and wanted to sink against him for comfort's sake. He didn't react, and she cleared her throat. "I can't believe she thought we were married."

"That was unexpected," he said. "I guess because we're here together."

"Probably. There's Gran's room."

"Looks like Grandpop is next door. See you in a bit."

Pulling in a fortifying breath, Vi knocked on the closed door. "Hi, Gran," she called out and opened it.

She noted an empty chair in the room. Gran lay propped up on a hospital bed, a blanket covering her. Unused equipment stood here and there, with a monitor tracking blood pressure, temperature and other things.

A look of sheer relief crossed her grandma's face. "You made good time. I'm glad to see you."

She didn't look too banged up, at least not to Vi. "Have you seen a doctor yet?"

"No, but a darling nurse is keeping an eye on me." She looked pale and exhausted.

"Are you in pain?" Vi asked.

"A headache. I hit my head. My arm hurts, too."

Oh, no. Vi hoped she didn't have a concussion. "What happened?"

"Malcom and I were in the car, and—"

"Fighting when you're driving is a bad idea."

"Fighting? We weren't even speaking to each other. And now…" Gran's eyes filled, and she bit her lip.

She'd never cried in front of Vi, and seeing her about to fall apart nearly broke her heart. "Neither you nor Malcom should drive when you're upset," she said as gently as she could. "Anyway, I thought he didn't drive at night."

"Remember, it wasn't close to dark when we arrived at the restaurant, and we left shortly after you did." Her hands twisted the corner of the blanket. "We shouldn't have fought that way, especially in public. What Malcom planned to do without a word to me was shocking. Then he yelled, and I let my temper get the better of me. By the way, remind me to thank Blake for paying for our dinner."

Vi nodded and prodded, "About the accident…"

"It wasn't Malcom's fault. A teenage boy driving around with his friends crashed into us."

"Oh, my God. Are they hurt, too?"

"They didn't need to come to the ER, so I doubt it. You should see Malcom's beautiful gold Mercedes. We think it's been totaled. His mechanic will let us know. The car has already been towed there. The boy called his parents and they came right over."

"How's Malcom?"

"He was able to arrange a tow of his car to the garage and talk with his insurance agent. But he's in pain, too. Terrible pain."

This was worrisome. Vi wondered how Blake was coping. Soon enough, she'd find out. "You called from his phone?"

"I left mine at home. Can you believe that?"

"How did you get here? Did you call Falcon Ride Service?"

For a moment, Gran looked puzzled. Then, "Ah, you mean the ride share company Malcom founded. We didn't have to. A nice policeman, Officer Noodling, helped us. Isn't that a funny name? He issued a ticket to the driver and checked both Malcom and me for injuries. He's the one who decided to bring us here."

"I'm so sorry, Gran, and I wish we hadn't left the restaurant when we did."

"Don't worry about that. It wouldn't have changed anything."

Gran closed her eyes, and Vi clenched her hands at her sides. "Are you okay?"

"I will be, once my head and arm stop hurting."

Vi sat in the empty chair. After over an hour with nothing happening, her patience snapped. Enough waiting for the doctor. She stood. "I'll be right back." As she reached the door to Gran's room, a sharp knock sounded and the door opened.

A man who couldn't have been much older than Vi strode in. Tall and thin, he looked like a gangly teen himself. "I'm Dr. Martin," he said. "How are you feeling, Mrs. Newberger?"

"Please, call me Caroline. My head hurts and so does my arm."

"The nurse told me. That's quite a bruise on your upper arm."

Vi hadn't noticed that. "I'm Vi Preston, Caroline's granddaughter," she told the doctor.

"Nice to meet you," he said and started a thorough

checkup on Gran. "I ordered a CT scan to make sure your head and neck are okay. Someone will be here shortly to take you upstairs where we do all that."

"While the doctor examines me, why don't you wait outside, Vi," Gran suggested.

"Okay. I'll stay nearby."

She stepped into the hallway and found Blake pacing around. "What's going on?" she asked. "Is Malcom okay?"

"He's getting his ribs x-rayed. The doctor wants to see if he broke something."

"That doesn't sound good."

"No, but otherwise, he seems okay. Except his right cheek. It's bruised and swollen. How's Caroline?"

As Vi updated him, a CT nurse wheeled Gran away to get her scan.

"Sounds like they'll both survive," Blake said.

"Let's hope. Did Malcom tell you what happened?"

"He didn't feel like talking."

"Here's what Gran said." She lowered her voice and filled him in.

"I'd like to give that kid a piece of my mind," he muttered.

"I'm sure his parents will do that. Whether or not the Mercedes is totaled, the family's insurance rates will skyrocket. I'm going to text my mother now, then call Rose and update her. She'll probably be asleep—it's two hours later in Mexico but she'd want to know. I'll leave a voice message."

He nodded. "Ditto with Whitney and my mother."

CHAPTER 10

It was nearing midnight when Blake got the okay to take Malcom home. Vi and Caroline were waiting for them, Caroline having been cleared a short time before Malcom. Both looked pretty banged up, but at least they were in decent enough shape to ride in the car.

Waiting for their discharge papers, the two of them gazed at each other with clear relief. "You have a bruise on your cheek," Caroline said, in a mournful voice. "Does it hurt? How are your ribs?"

"I hurt like the devil. One rib is cracked and will take several weeks to heal up. How are your head and arm?"

"The arm is sore but nothing I can't live with. I also have a minor concussion and a headache. What a pair we are." She moved closer to him and peered at his face. "You don't look so good."

"Neither do you. We both need to get some sleep."

"Be sure to get enough rest, drink plenty of water, and take aspirin as needed," the nurse advised as she handed them their medical instructions. "The doctor would like you to contact your primary care physicians for full exams."

Grandpop wasn't the best at following instructions, but Blake intended to make sure he paid attention to that. "I'll schedule an appointment first thing tomorrow, and I'll drive you there and back." He wasn't sure how he'd squeeze in the time to do that, but his grandfather's health was more important than either bike store.

"You're a busy man. I don't mind calling Falcon."

"I want to take you. Let's get you two home."

With the ER so close to the 709, the trip wouldn't take long. Malcom sat gingerly in front with Blake, Vi and Caroline in the back.

"I'll bet you're both tired," Vi said in the silence.

"Yes, it's been a long night. This is a nice car, Blake. Almost as nice as the Mercedes is—or was." He heard Caroline shifting around. "I'm sitting on something back here that's uncomfortable."

"I can't imagine what," Vi said. "Whatever it is, I'll get it out of the way. Can you lift up a little? Oh," she said a few seconds later. Blake glanced in the rearview mirror to see her clutching something in her hand.

"What is that?" Caroline asked.

"It's a hairbrush."

"Is it Blake's?"

"No, mine."

"Well, what's it doing in the back seat?"

"Um…" Long pause. "I didn't realize it was missing from my purse."

Not an answer, and Caroline went quiet. Blake thought sure Vi had shoved it into her bag after she'd fixed her hair.

Not that he'd paid much attention. Blame that on the powerful kisses they'd traded. "How'd it get back there?" he asked, feigning ignorance.

"I have no idea," Vi answered. He guessed she was blushing and was glad for the darkness hiding it.

"Can't think of a good answer, is that it?" Grandpop said. "Don't bother—us old people weren't born yesterday. We'd know if you tried to feed us any bull. Here's what I think— you pulled the brush from your purse and it dropped on the seat. You were in the back and I'm pretty sure Blake was there with you." Grandpop stroked his chin as if in deep thought. "Now, what could you two have been doing in the back seat before you strolled into the restaurant?"

Blake was momentarily struck speechless. Vi, too, was silent. "Where did you come up with that idea?" he finally managed. He wasn't about to explain about Vi's bad case of nerves or the massage he'd given her to help, and for sure not going near those kisses that'd all but wiped his mind clean of anything else.

"Console in your way, was it?"

Damn, the man was sharp. He never missed anything. "Cut it out, Grandpop," he warned.

"I knew it!" Gran chimed out in the silence. "Vi was flushed when you two came in. And a good ten minutes late, which she rarely is. And Blake, explaining that the color in her face was due to the cold. You're a clever one, not so different from your grandfather."

"Stop it, both of you," Vi ordered in a no-nonsense tone.

Grandpop ignored her. "You kids didn't waste any time, you pair of chips off the old block." He cackled, then abruptly broke off and groaned. "It hurts when I laugh."

The pair of chips off the blocks comment made no sense, and Blake slanted the man a curious frown. He wasn't about to ask about it, though. Why give the man a chance to say more of what he didn't want to hear?

They pulled into the parking lot of the 709, and the conversation turned to getting Malcom and Caroline out of the car. Inside, they greeted the night staff person, who'd been briefed about the situation.

The four of them rode the elevator to the sixth floor. Blake helped Grandpop to his room, a slow process due to the pain, and Vi took care of Caroline. By the time he got Grandpop settled with water and aspirin tabs within reach and a button to notify the medical staff if he needed help, which, of course, the man stubbornly resisted, he was more than ready to take Vi home and crash.

As soon as she stepped into the lobby, they left.

WORN out after the traumatic events of the evening, Vi yawned as Blake pulled onto the highway and drove toward the townhouse. "This is a night I won't soon forget."

"You can say that about the entire day."

By his quick glance at her mouth, she knew what he was referring to. "I nearly keeled over in embarrassment when Malcom talked about my brush being in the back seat. How did that lead to his figuring out exactly what we did?"

"I wasn't happy about it, either, but it was pretty funny." His lips twitched.

He had a point. "Looking back, I get that. Now, anyway."

They shared a smile, and Blake went on. "Knowing him, he

figured you're a female, I'm a male, and we were alone together in the car. We wanted to fool around where we had more room."

"That's not why we were in the back."

"He didn't know that."

"I wasn't going to say I was desperate to calm down and you needed space to work on my neck and shoulders. To clear up any misunderstanding, I had no intention of kissing you more than once as a gesture of gratitude." She doubted he would've kissed her in the first place if she hadn't been so impulsive.

"You're not attracted to me?" He sounded disappointed.

"Of course, I am. You're a good kisser," *very* good, "but don't let that go to your head. It doesn't mean I expected us to go on the way we did." She frowned at him. "You're smiling again."

"Because you're attracted to me," he said, gloating like he'd won a prize.

Men. "And that makes you happy? I have no idea why, when we both know the feeling isn't mutual."

"It sure as heck is."

She was flattered but not stupid. "Come on, Blake, there are tons of women out there more your type." Ready to talk about something else, she changed the subject. "You won't believe what Gran said when we were alone."

"Hold that a minute. Tell me, what's my type?"

No need even to think about that. "Gorgeous, sexy, fun."

"You're describing yourself."

She narrowed her eyes his way. "Stop with the phony compliments. I know my limits."

"Enlighten me and tell me what they are."

"I don't have much of a sense of humor, I'm not curvy, I'm too smart," she rattled off. Stuff she'd been mocked for in middle school and high school.

"Where did you come up with that load of crap?"

Not about to get into the thorny details, she eyed him. "Do you want to know what Gran said or not?"

"Hit me."

"She said what we did in the back seat was a lot like her and Malcom when they first met. Instant attraction and us not being able to keep our hands off each other. Puh-lease." Which in her case, like it or not, was true.

"That explains the crack he made about us being double chips off the old block." Blake snorted. "Not. I'm nowhere near ready to get married."

"On that, we agree. I'd like to someday, but I've never even come close to meeting anyone I want to spend my life with. With parents like ours, is it any wonder?" Vi clapped her hand over her mouth. "I had no business saying that. I mean like mine."

"You're right about my family, too. My mother, at least. I almost got married once."

Surprised, she gawked at him. "What happened?"

"We realized we'd made a mistake and parted ways."

What kind of mistake, and how long ago? She wanted to know but wasn't going to ask, as she didn't want to seem nosy. "Our grandparents have seen each other angry, I'll bet for the first time. Between that and the accident, maybe they'll table their plan to get married and come to the realization that like you and your ex, they're making a mistake and need more time."

"Hard to know what they'll do. We still ought to figure out what our next steps are."

For a moment, Vi thought he meant between them. Fatigue was messing with her mind. He was talking about Gran and Malcom. She didn't want to think about Blake except as an ally wanting to stop their grandparents from rushing into anything. "Next steps." She scoffed at the idea. "You saw how well that worked out at dinner tonight. At the moment, I'm too brain-dead to think about that or anything else. Let's wait and see how they feel over the next day or two."

"I'm surprised—you're not a wait and see person."

"Yeah, well I learned that with Gran and Malcom, we have no other choice."

He cupped his ear. "Did I hear you right, and you agree with me?"

"Just this once," she teased.

"I'll check in after I take Grandpop to the doctor, and you do the same."

Signaling, he turned into the complex. As he pulled up in front of her unit, she tensed. He'd better not try anything. When he didn't, she was both relieved and oddly disappointed. His car idled there until she unlocked the door and let herself in. Then he drove off.

CHAPTER 11

Between taking Grandpop to his doctor's appointment, getting the new bike shop in shape and keeping tabs on the original store, Blake was too busy during the week to do more than exchange a quick email or two with Vi. She seemed equally busy. Both of them checked in with their grandparents daily. Grandpop was focused on his bruised rib and the swelling and discoloring there and on his cheek. He didn't talk about anything else. According to Vi, the discussion with Caroline was much the same.

As busy as Blake was, he often thought about Vi. Brief emails only said so much. How was she doing at work? Mostly though, he thought about other things. The sweetness of her hand in his when he'd needed it. The eager taste of her lips. The prissy hairdo she wore when she was at work, and the swishy ponytail otherwise.

He'd known her exactly one week, but with everything that'd happened it felt much longer. Small wonder, the way their grandparents put them through an emotional wringer.

She was outspoken but not obnoxious, intelligent, and an all-around decent person. She'd been standoffish at first, but that had quickly faded. She came across as a confident woman, and yet... He couldn't get over her opinion that she was average when she was beautiful and hot.

Meanwhile, he was on-edge. Were his grandfather and Caroline still mad at each other, or had they broken up since their fight? Heck if he knew. He hadn't heard a thing about that from the man, and according to Vi, Caroline was also mum on the subject. Best to let each of them alone with their thoughts.

Except the silence was killing him. No doubt, Vi was in the same boat. He'd grown frustrated waiting the man out. To hell with that. Time to pay a visit to the 709 and get the real scoop, then contact Vi and share what he learned.

But on the way to the retirement home, he changed his mind and decided to drop by her place instead. After a quick visit to the grocery and a nearby diner, he headed for the townhouse.

* * *

BY FRIDAY, sick of the long hours and ready to wind down and forget work for a while, Vi left the office at five o'clock. Once home, she considered various options. Seeing a movie with Carmie sounded fun—if she didn't have plans with Chris. Treating herself to dinner someplace, and then doing the movie thing solo would be okay, or scrounging up something to eat at home, sipping wine while watching the tube, then falling into bed for a much-needed long night's sleep.

Undecided, she poured a glass of wine and sat down to think about it. The doorbell chimed. Who could that be? She frowned. Rose wasn't due back till the following evening. Maybe one of the neighbors needed to borrow an egg or a cup of sugar. She'd done that a time or two herself.

The last person she expected to see on the front stoop was Blake. In jeans, a faded denim jacket and a slate-blue Henley shirt that brought out the navy color of his piercing eyes, he looked yummy enough to—Vi shut off the thought. She was *not* going to drool over a man she had no business getting involved with. "Hi, there. What brings you here?" she asked, happier to see him than was wise.

"It's Friday night, I'm tired, and I want to hang with someone who's going through the same hell as me. That'd be you. Besides, we haven't talked for a week, and the texting is getting old."

Of course, the thing with the grandparents. Nothing remotely romantic in that. Which was good, though deep down a part of her wanted him to be interested in her romantically, even if it did spell trouble.

She shoved the blasphemous thought from her mind just as he held up a bag from McPherson's, a popular diner, and threw her an irresistible grin. "I brought sustenance. Gonna let me in?"

"McPherson's—yum," she said, salivating as he stepped inside. "I love that place. What all did you get?"

He handed her the bag and shrugged out of his jacket. The shirt was long-sleeve and oh, my, those broad shoulders and flat belly. She couldn't help but remember the feel of his body so close the other night… She swallowed hard.

"First, I stopped at Collingwood's Grocery for a bottle of wine," he said, thankfully oblivious to her admiration. "Then I picked up two orders of fried chicken, mashed potatoes with a side of gravy, and green beans. They packed it piping hot, but it's cooled off a bit and should be heated before we eat—that is, if you haven't had dinner yet."

"I haven't, and I'm hungry. It smells really good."

"Music to my ears. Let's—" Mr. T sashayed toward him. He stopped what he was saying and crouched down. "Hey there, buddy," he said, and rubbed the area on the tom's back just above his tail. Loud purring ensued.

"He likes you," Vi said, and so did she. "I just opened a bottle of wine, so save yours for another time. Give me that food, pour yourself a glass from the open bottle, and I'll start the microwaving."

Man and cat followed her into the kitchen. She pointed out the cabinet with the wine glasses and set to work. While the food heated, she handed plates and silverware to Blake. Moments later, the kitchen filled with the smells of fried chicken and gravy.

"Oh, the aroma," she said and licked her lips. "You took a big chance stopping by without calling first." Normally, she preferred advance notice and the chance to say no thanks, but she was really happy to see him and the food. "What if I'd made dinner for myself?"

"C'mon, Vi, don't frown at me, not after all we've been through. You're right, I should've phoned. It was a spur-of-the moment thing. We haven't had a chance to talk since the accident. I figured we'd eat while we caught up. Don't I get points for bringing dinner?"

Wearing an earnest and innocent expression, he was irresistible. "I'll forgive you this once," she said, adding a grumble for effect.

He flashed another charming grin, and she had a hunch he got away with pulling stuff like this with other women he dated. But she wasn't dating him, she reminded herself. Far from it. She wasn't about to fall under his spell and get involved like that, only to be dumped when he moved on.

"What's the latest at DD Telecom?" he asked as they sat down at the eating counter.

He would bring that up. "Please, not that, just when I'm ready to dig in. In a nutshell, it's a mess, and you know how I love that." She paused to sip her wine. "We're all working long hours without much to show for it."

He squinted at her. "If you don't take care of yourself, you'll get sick."

"Who has time for that?" She sighed. "What you mean is, I look tired. It's true, I'm running myself ragged, and I'm not the only one. Things are so bad, I don't know how much longer any of us can continue to work at this pace. I'm doing everything I can to help, but I feel like Sisyphus, pushing a heavy rock up a steep hill, only to have it roll to the bottom again."

"Sounds brutal. What about finding a new job?"

"I've thought about that, but I love this company. I'm determined to hang on and do what I do while it struggles to right itself. How are things at the bike shop?"

"Busy, but nothing like your situation. After a few rough starts, things are coming together pretty much on schedule. Wait'll you see it. Which reminds me, our grand opening is the first day of May. That's a Wednesday. You're invited."

"Thanks. I'll try to make it—if I'm still standing." She

managed a slight smile. "I'll add it to my calendar right now, before I forget. What time?"

"It's an all-day thing, starting at nine a.m. and ending eight p.m. Stop by when you can. I'm running ads on social media, the Port Simms Weekly and the radio, and offering a discount on rentals and purchases made during the first week. Ross, the cycling buddy I told you about the other day, is doing a decent job interviewing and hiring. That's a big load off my shoulders. He mentioned wanting to stay on, but he tends to change jobs frequently, and I don't want to end up in another situation of losing my HR person."

"He sounds like Rose. She switches a lot, too, but she doesn't really have to work. Her husband Peter is a hotshot surgeon and makes plenty of money."

"I'll bet." They finished the meal. "It won't get dark for a while and it's still nice outside. Let's take a walk."

"What a great idea," Vi said. "I've pretty much been inside since Monday morning. Why don't I show you around?"

"I saw the play area and a few other places when I was here before, but I wouldn't mind seeing them again."

"I meant outside the complex. There's a park nearby and a lot of cute little shops. Why don't we take a look?" As they headed toward the park, Vi marveled at the changes in the landscape over the past week. "Suddenly, flowers are budding and blooming everywhere. The air smells so good. Without this walk I would've missed it, and spring is one of my favorite seasons of the year." She gave Blake a grateful smile. "This is exactly what I needed."

"There's that beautiful smile. I'm thinking about dessert. Is that an Ice Creamery down and across the street?"

"Sure is." Very much in the mood for ice cream, she hurried to the crosswalk. "Let's go before the light turns."

Blake reached for her hand much as he had the other night. "C'mon, it's about to change."

Did he have to do that? It only made her like him more, the opposite of what she wanted. "I can get across the street without you holding my hand," she scolded and reclaimed it.

He seemed nonplussed. "Guess I got used to us grabbing on to each other the night of the accident. My apologies." She nodded, and they headed toward the shop. "The other day my mother called from the ashram. That was unexpected—she's not supposed to use the phone except in emergencies.

"I mentioned texting her the night of the accident. I did it again the next day about Grandpop's cracked rib, and that the doctor assured him and me he'd heal. She was worried anyway. I reassured her and said he'd be happy to hear from her. But like I said, she's not supposed to take time away from whatever it is she's doing. Before we hung up, I also told her about Caroline. She was surprised."

"I'll bet. I talked to my mom, too. Like yours, she wanted more info about the accident than she got through my text. I gave her the details and told her about Gran and Malcom and that I have no idea if they're still mad at each other or whether they'll go through with the marriage. She didn't comment about that and said she'd give Gran a call, but I don't know that she did. I'm sure Gran would tell me, or maybe not. Lately, all she talks about is her bruised arm. No more headache, which is a relief."

"That's good news. Except for health updates, they're not telling us much."

They went into the Ice Creamery and came out with

double-scoop cones. "This was a great idea," Vi said as she licked the caramel swirl scoop on top, then the midnight chocolate underneath. She realized Blake was staring at her. "Do I have ice cream on my face?"

"A little on your chin. It's cute."

He thought she was cute? For all of two seconds, she felt warm inside. Then reason kicked in. Fat chance. He probably said similar things to the women he actually dated. Stuffing the unwanted warmth deep inside, she dabbed at her chin with a napkin. "Better?" He nodded. "Gran has exactly two weeks left before she has to pay up or leave. My friend Carmie works for Port Simms Apartment Rentals. I'm going to talk to her about finding a place for Gran to stay."

"Wasn't she going to cash in her life insurance policy?"

"So she said, but I have no idea. When I brought it up on the phone the other day, she changed the subject. I also asked about a good time to come visit. She didn't want me taking time off from work especially now, and told me not to come. Then she ended the call." Vi compressed her lips. "It's so frustrating."

"Tell me about it. Grandpop's only interested in talking about his sore rib and bruised cheek, and how the second store is coming along."

"They're both deflecting our questions. I'm thinking they're embarrassed about the public fight. Although Gran sort of apologized and wanted you to know she thanks you for treating them to dinner. Either they have too much pride to admit to us they were wrong about their feelings for each other, or they're up to something and keeping it from us."

"Funny, I've been thinking about the same things. Great

minds... Hard to know which is the truth. My money's on the latter."

"Knowing how we feel about their quick decision to get married, that makes sense."

By the time they finished their cones, the sun was setting. "Let's head back before it's dark," Vi said. "I'm tired enough to fall asleep super early."

"A good night's rest will do you a world of good." He started to grasp hold of her, seemed to catch himself, and stuffed both hands into the pockets of his jeans jacket instead.

Smart man. "Since we don't know the reason is for their refusal to talk about their relationship, we need to find out." Vi tapped her finger to her lips while she thought about that. "Phone calls aren't working, but I'll bet if we visit in person we'll learn more. I haven't seen Gran since her doctor's appointment, and I really should. I'll stop by tomorrow whether or not she likes it. Rose gets back in the evening and I know Gran wants to see her, but it'll be too late to visit then. Anyway, I'm sure she and Peter will want to spend time together first."

"Sounds reasonable. I was going to visit Malcom tonight for the same reasons. I may as well do that tomorrow."

"Why didn't you see him tonight?"

"I wanted to see you."

He fixed an avid gaze on her, and she got all flustered. Darn the man for messing with her feelings and making her want what she shouldn't. "I don't think we should see them together or go to the 709 at the same time. If we stick to one-on-one conversations, they might be more willing to talk. If that doesn't work, we'll keep a close look on body language and facial expressions and do our best to puzzle out what they're not saying. I'm planning to sleep in tomorrow, so I'll come after lunch."

"I'll go in the morning before I meet with Ross for lunch and a summary of the past week's interviews. After our visits, you and I should compare notes."

"And we have a plan," she said, pleased.

"Without a single detail. On the way to dinner the other night, that bothered you a lot."

"Still does, but it can't be helped. We'll have to feel our way around them as we go."

He seemed surprised. "You're okay with that?"

"I don't have a choice."

"And look how easily we figured this out." He beamed at her. "We make a terrific team."

Was he trying to make her want him even more?

They reached the complex and soon arrived at her door. "Thanks for dinner, and for the walk," she said, looking forward to falling into bed.

"Back at ya for the ice cream."

She pulled the key from her jacket pocket and unlocked the door. She was about to open it and let herself in when Blake leaned in and kissed her. *Not again.* But instead of pushing him away, she clutched his jacket lapels and kissed him back. The key dropped from her fingers. The clanking sound on the concrete step brought her to her senses. *Stop.*

Frowning, she picked it up. "Why did you do that?"

"I needed more of something sweet—you. Kissing you is better than any ice cream."

Laughter bubbled out of her. "How did I not know what a cornball you are?" She wanted to remind him that his flattery didn't affect her in the least, but blurted out something else. "Do it again."

She considered taking the words back and reminding him she had no interest in being one more name on the list of women he'd seduced, but his clever mouth teasing her lips erased the thought. Her body hummed with longing she couldn't stop and didn't want to. Outside where anyone could see.

She opened the door and yanked him inside.

CHAPTER 12

Inside Vi's house, Blake kicked the door shut, shrugged out of his jacket while she did the same, pulled her into his arms and went back to kissing her. She tasted even sweeter than before. Her lips eagerly meeting his with growing passion, the feel of her soft body in his arms... He couldn't get enough. Craving deeper kisses, he slid his tongue into her mouth. With a soft moan, she pressed closer, her body tight against his. Killing him. He cupped her hips to anchor her there. "I want you."

As soon as he uttered the words, she stiffened as if he'd poured a bucket of cold water on her and pushed him away.

"We have to stop, Blake. This isn't right."

The words didn't match her enthusiasm or the restless way she'd shimmied against him. He let go of her and stepped back. "It feels right to me, but I get it—we're moving too fast. I didn't mean for that to happen, but I can't lie. You turn me on." Her cheeks were flushed, her lips slightly red from the passionate kissing and her hair loose and messy, and he hungered to get right back to it.

"I don't want to turn you on, and I don't want to be turned on."

"You were, though. We both were."

Mr. T sashayed toward them and twined himself between her ankles. "Fine watch cat you are," she grumbled. "Why did you kiss me this time, Blake?"

"Truthfully, I've been thinking about it on and off since the last time. But I didn't plan anything, I swear. It just happened. I enjoyed spending the past few hours with you and commiserating over the situation with our grandparents. A goodnight kiss is customary after a date."

"This was *not* a date," she stated with heat in her voice.

"Your mixed messages are confusing. One minute you're warm and friendly and step eagerly into my arms. A few hot kisses later, you tell me you don't want to date and act like you're ticked off."

"You came over uninvited to talk about a shared problem. I appreciated the food and I enjoyed the walk and the ice cream. I thought we were friends. Other than that, I don't want to get involved with you."

Too late. "The way I see it, we've moved beyond simple friendship. I agree, we got involved more quickly than usual, but this is how we are together. It's as much your fault as mine. I gave you a chaste good night kiss. You wanted more and hauled me into the house."

"I didn't want the neighbors to talk, okay? The same thing happened in the back seat of your car, only you did the pulling. It was wrong both times, a mistake."

"Was it? You can't deny the chemistry between us."

She covered her hands with her ears for a few seconds, as if not wanting to hear another word about it. "I'm not some gullible female, and I don't want to be seduced, especially by you."

Especially him? What did she think he was, anyway? He started to ask her to explain, but her dirty look and crossed arms silenced him.

"By your clueless expression, you want me to clarify." An exasperated breath huffed out. "All right, I will. You flit from woman to woman. That's your choice, but I refuse to be one of them. Not again. Now please, go."

She opened the door and ushered him out.

As tired as Vi was, she slept badly. She woke up way too early, thinking about the night before. Getting tangled up in Blake's arms and melting into his kisses. She was furious about losing herself with him. If only she could go back and end the evening with the light kiss at the door and stepping into the house alone. Then she wouldn't be reliving everything and craving more.

She gave him mixed messages, he'd said. In the light of day, she realized he was right. As torn as she was between steering clear and wanting him, was it any wonder? She didn't understand herself at all or have any idea how he felt about her, except that she turned him on. It stopped now. She intended to forget all about the fire sparking between them and hoped he would, too.

If Gran and Malcom decided to part ways, she wouldn't have to see or talk to Blake. Please, let that be the case. For now, like it or not, they were stuck having to deal with their grandparents together. Why did she ache for Blake when he wasn't at all what she wanted? He enjoyed playing the field. She didn't do that, was looking for someone with a heart of gold who was true blue to the woman he cared about. Was that asking too much?

Maybe it was, and like Gran said, her standards were impossibly high.

In need of advice, she texted Carmie. *Want to talk. Meet in an hour at the Hastings between where we live?*

Good friend that she was the reply came right away. *Chris just left my place—he has to work today, but I don't. How about an hour from now?*

Perfect. Hastings was busy, as it usually was on a Saturday morning. A couple about her age were leaving, and she set her jacket on the back of a chair to reserve the table. Then she joined the line of people waiting to order.

Things moved slowly, and Vi people watched. Two college-age guys in front of her talked about their plans for the evening. "I really like this girl," one said to the other.

"Cool. What's your next move?"

"To take my time. I don't want to mess up my chances by moving too fast."

"Wow, you must more than like her."

"I do. She could be the one."

Vi sighed. Just once, it'd be nice to meet someone like that, a man who thought she was *The One* and they decided together to move slowly enough to make sure they were right for each other. With Blake, it was like a forest fire raging through water-starved trees.

"Hey, you," Carmie called out from behind her. There were three people between them. "Come back here with me."

116

The woman directly behind Vi smiled. "Why don't you come up here with your friend? I don't mind."

"That's so nice—thanks," Vi said, and Carmie joined her. "I got us a table over there by the bookcase. I haven't eaten yet. The ham and cheese croissants look good."

"I had a bowl of cereal but could go for a muffin."

Moments later, they took their coffees and food to the table.

"Chris invited me to Sweet Sue's next Friday night," Carmie announced as soon as they sat down.

"Now, that's news." The classy restaurant in the upscale area downtown was especially popular for celebrations and other special occasions. Vi smiled. "He must have something important to discuss with you."

"You mean like a proposal? Fingers and toes crossed."

"But not our eyes," Vi said and laughed at her own words.

Carmie laughed, too, then nibbled her muffin and studied her. "I'm glad you texted this morning. We haven't seen each other in a while. What's up with you?"

Vi started with the easiest topic—work. "It's been insane all week, but surely things will settle down soon. I haven't changed my mind about looking for a new job. If I stick around and wait for the dust to clear, I'll be in a good position for the promotion I want."

"They'd better pay you the bonus you're owed, too. What's going on with your grandma and her boyfriend? Are they recovering after the car accident?"

"They seem to be. The problem is, Gran hasn't mentioned Malcom to me, and Malcom doesn't say a word about her to Blake. We can't figure out if they're still mad at each other or if they made plans they don't want us to know about. Which reminds me. If they decide not to get married and she wants to leave the 709, she'll need a place to rent. Do you think you can find her something reasonably priced?

"I can try. What will she want in an apartment?"

"I don't know—we haven't discussed that."

"When you figure it out, let me know and I'll get to work. Why don't you ask her? Blake should do the same with his grandpa and find out his opinion on the matter."

"We've been waiting for them to tell us on their own. Neither of them is exactly flexible, and we don't want to get on their bad sides. Our hopes are that they'll tell us when they're ready."

"If they don't?"

"We'll keep strategizing." The thought of her and Blake figuring out what to do together tied Vi up in knots. She wasn't at all sure she wanted to see or talk to him.

"You look like you swallowed a bug," Carmie said. "What's wrong?"

"I'm a mess. I have so much to tell you." Vi lowered her voice and shared about the kisses both in Blake's car and the previous night.

Carmie smiled and shook her head. "You two don't waste any time."

Vi set the croissant down and wiped her fingers with her napkin. "Both times were a mistake. Blake mentioned that he dates a lot of women and hasn't had many girlfriends. He was engaged once, but he and his then fiancée called off the wedding."

"He's honest. That's good."

Vi agreed. "From what he says, he doesn't stay with a

woman for long. I don't want to be another female he sweet talks into bed and then moves on to someone else."

"Hey, you do the same thing."

"Not sexually. I happen to be testing the waters and trying to find the right person."

"Pot calling the kettle?"

"No way. Blake's a player. I'm not."

"I get the feeling his behavior reminds you of Devin. If you know that, why mess around with him?"

"I ask myself the same question. The truth is, he's not easy to resist."

"So that's how it is. What's your plan?"

"After we finish dealing with the grandparents thing, I'll stop seeing him." And meanwhile, keep a respectable distance from him, no matter how challenging it was.

"When do you think that will be?"

"Soon, I hope. Blake's visiting his grandfather now. I'm going to stop in at Gran's in an hour or so. We'll compare notes and go from there." Staying well out of touching distance. "Wish us luck."

CHAPTER 13

As soon as Blake opened his eyes Saturday morning, he thought about Vi's parting words the night before. *You flit from one woman to another, and I refuse to be one of them. Not again.* She made him sound like a real jerk who dated women solely to get them into bed. He liked sex but wasn't like that and never had been. What made her think he was?

From what she hinted at, he figured some creep had treated her that way. Not him, ever. He needed to set her straight and would when they met up later in the day.

When he was almost at the 709, he phoned Grandpop and let him know he was coming.

His grandfather answered in his usual terse voice. "Blake."

Not wanting the man to tell him not to come, he kept the call short. "I'm on my way to visit and will be at your place in five."

After he parked and signed in, he rode the elevator up, then knocked at the door.

"Come in," Grandpop said. He was seated in his La-Z-Boy facing the TV with a scowl on his face. Not in a good mood, then. The bruise on his cheek looked almost as nasty as it had the day after the accident, and he was still a little pale. Pain was a real mood downer.

Wanting to cheer him up, Blake showed him a bag. "I brought you a treat. Lox, bagels and cream cheese, a favorite of yours. There are two here, one for today and another for tomorrow."

The old eyes lit up and an almost-smile chased away the scowl. The remote was on a TV tray in front of him, and he shut off the tube. "How did you know I haven't eaten?"

"It's early yet, and you don't keep the morning hours you used to. I'll put the extra bagel in the fridge and get you a plate and something to drink. Water okay?"

The man nodded. "You'll find a carton of orange juice on the top shelf of the fridge. Bring that, too."

After arranging everything on the TV tray, Blake sat down on the nearby sofa while his grandfather ate. "That's one heck of a bruise on your cheek, but you're not as pale as you were when I took you to the doctor last week," he said. "How's the rib?"

"You ask me that every time you call. Same as I told you on the phone yesterday. I still hurt when I move around, but I'll get better and the rib should stop bothering me in three to four weeks. What brings you here?"

"I haven't seen you since I took you to the doctor almost a week ago and wanted to visit."

"If you'd called ahead, I'd have said don't bother and saved you the trip. You're busy getting that new store ready to go, and this is a waste of your time. I'm not in the best mood."

No kidding. "You're welcome, Grandpop. Glad you appreciate the fact that I drove out of my way to bring you the lox and bagel."

"Thanks," came the grudging reply. "Why are you really here?"

Grouchy or not, he was too perceptive for his own good. "Since you asked, I want to know what's going on with you and Caroline. You haven't mentioned her."

Grandpop's expression soured even more. "You haven't asked. It's obvious you disapprove of our relationship."

"I like Caroline," Blake replied. He'd like her even better if she and his grandfather weren't talking marriage. "I'm asking now."

"She's still mad at me."

The other reason beside pain making him out of sorts. "After a whole week? That's not good."

"Think I don't know that?"

"What did she say when you talked to her about it?"

"I haven't."

"Don't you think it's time you did?"

"I don't know, all right? Now, let me eat in peace. And don't sit here staring at me. The coffee maker's set up. Why don't you make some for both of us."

Blake stood and started the brewing, then returned to the sofa. When most of the bagel had disappeared some minutes later, he cleared away the dishes and loaded them in the dishwasher. "Have you changed your mind about Caroline?" he asked as he filled two mugs.

"What kind of question is that? Quit talking and bring me that coffee."

Half wishing he'd stayed away and stifling the urge to lose

his cool, Blake set the drink on the tray and brought his to the sofa. "Do you still care about Caroline?"

"'Course I do!" Grandpop winced. "Hurts when I yell."

"I'll bet. Have you considered apologizing to her?"

"For wanting to surprise her with a generous wedding gift most women would happily accept? She ought to be apologizing to me." He raised his chin in stubborn defiance, yet for all his bravado, he looked old and defeated.

As much as Blake wanted his grandfather and Caroline to at least back away from the marriage idea, he hated seeing him like this. For a man who'd been married for decades, he didn't seem to know much about women. "I'm no expert, but if I liked a woman as much as you like Caroline and wanted to right a wrong, I'd ease up on the stubbornness. A heartfelt apology can go a long way to heal the problems between you."

"I'm not stubborn, and I didn't do anything wrong," Grandpop insisted, proving exactly how stubborn he was. "How was I to know she'd get mad about her present?"

"Hey, you found out she doesn't like that kind of surprise. Also, she wants to pay her own way. In my book, that's admirable. Maybe you should've listened to her."

"Stop lecturing me, boy. What the hell am I to do?"

Blake had already shared his opinion, but he repeated it. "If I were in your shoes, I'd give in and apologize. But if you believe she's in the wrong and you're in the right, then I don't see a way to fix this."

Grandpop clamped his lips, picked up the remote and turned the TV back on, effectively dismissing the conversation and Blake. His way of saying he wanted to be alone and think things out.

"Time for me to go—I have a meeting," Blake said and stood. "See you again soon, Grandpop."

* * *

BLAKE'S TEXT arrived when Vi was pulling into the 709. *Meeting with Grandpop didn't go well. Text or call after you see Caroline.*

Big help that was. When she signed in, she noted he'd left ten minutes earlier.

She called Gran with a quick, "Surprise! I'm on my way up to see you." Quickly disconnecting, she headed up the elevator.

"Come in," Gran called out when she knocked at the door. She was sitting on the couch with the Port Simms Weekly paper and greeted Vi with a touch of irritation. "You're lucky I was here. What if I'd been out and missed you?" She patted the seat beside her. "Sit."

"Sorry, Gran. I should've called earlier." Would've, if she'd thought the woman wouldn't try to put her off. She squinted at her. "Have you lost weight?"

"I don't know. Why, do I look thinner?"

"Yes. Is something wrong with the food here?"

Gran shook her head. "I don't have much appetite."

Possible reasons for that skittered through Vi's mind. Diabetes, maybe cancer, or any number of other illnesses. "I don't like that, Gran."

"Whatever you're worried about, stop. I have plenty of padding. For your information, I had an early lunch today, and I ate very well." Gran yawned. "What time does Rose get home?"

"Tonight. I don't know exactly when. I'm sure she'll be in touch tomorrow. Who'd you have lunch with?" Vi asked, wondering if Malcom felt well enough to sit in the dining room. Gran hadn't said, and neither had the text from Blake.

"Two of my new friends, Suzanne and Karen. They're easy to talk to and make me laugh. You'd like them. I'll introduce you sometime."

Not a word about Malcom. Hmm...

Gran eyed the box Vi had brought from Melissa Ann's Bakery. "What's in there?"

"Two banana cinnamon muffins with chocolate chips. I hope you still have room for one."

"You know me better than that. Hand over that box. I'll get plates and napkins for both of us."

She felt well enough to eat her treat, a good sign. "None for me, Gran. I had a croissant earlier. These are for you."

Her grandma took a generous bite. "This is so good. Thanks, Vi. You've always been a thoughtful girl—er woman."

Another yawn followed. Come to think of it, she looked tired as well as thinner. Fatigue and the circles under her eyes added years to her. Vi was concerned. "Are you taking anything for the pain, Gran?"

"Don't need to. I feel pretty good. My bruise is ugly, but it should begin to fade soon. I told you that when you phoned yesterday. Don't you remember?"

"Of course, but I couldn't see you then. It's obvious you're worn out. What's keeping you up at night? Are you still traumatized about the car accident?"

Emotions Vi couldn't read flitted across the weathered face. "The accident has nothing to do with it." Gran set the muffin aside. "I'm too mad to sleep or eat."

"Oh?" Vi asked, guessing things were still awry with Malcom. "What's bothering you?"

"I don't want to talk about it." Glancing away, Gran sniffed and dabbed her eyes with her napkin.

Was she tearing up? Vi had only seen her cry once, shortly after Gramps had passed away years earlier. "Talk to me, Gran."

Her face still averted, she shook her head. The misery likely had to do with Malcom. It seemed they were still mad at each other. Vi assumed Blake had met with the same headstrong refusal from his grandfather to discuss the problem. Knowing she couldn't force the issue, she changed the subject. "You have two weeks left to decide about the 709. Are you planning to stay, and if not, where do you want to live? Carmie can help us find a nice apartment for you. But if you're positive about staying here, will it be in this unit, or are you and Malcom going to share a place?"

At last, her grandma turned toward her. The sorrowful expression on her face made Vi's chest ache.

"I have no idea what Malcom wants. He certainly hasn't apologized for lying to me about paying my share of the down payment on the new unit. Honesty is very important to me. I don't know if I can forgive him for that." She rested her head in her hands and sniffled loudly.

"Gran, are you all right?"

"How could I be? I love him and miss him so much. Does that make me a fool?"

Vi was confused. "You two haven't spoken?"

"Not since the day after the accident. We compared notes on our doctor's appointments, and that was it."

"Why aren't you talking?"

"That happened when I let him know I expected an apology. He said I should apologize to him instead of getting angry. The only reason he didn't shout at me was because yelling hurts his rib. Oh, that man!"

As mad as Gran was, tears continued to stream down her face. Vi tried to squeeze her hand, but was rebuffed. "What are you going to do?"

Looking sad, heartbroken and stubborn all at once, Gran crossed her arms. "Nothing. He was in the wrong—he should apologize."

"What if he doesn't?" Vi asked in a soft voice.

"It's his loss."

Gran blew her nose and seemed so forlorn that Vi half-wished the couple would make up. "Maybe it's time to move into an apartment."

"I like living here too much to let him chase me out."

"But with Malcom just down the hall, you're bound to run into each other either up here or downstairs during cocktail hour or in the dining room. It'll be awkward and uncomfortable."

"I'm not a child, Vi. I know how to be civil. I'll get used to it."

"Then you're staying right here, in this unit?"

"That's right. The insurance check hasn't arrived yet. I expected it sometime this past week, but I'm sure it'll be here any day now. I'll check with the insurance company Monday morning."

Did Malcom know about this? Did he even care? Vi was anxious to talk to Blake and compare notes. Yet she had to offer. "Do you want me to sit with you for a while?"

Gran shook her head. "I'm blue, but I'm all right."

CHAPTER 14

Blake was finishing the meeting with Ross when Vi called. "I'm about to leave the 709. My meeting with Gran was so sad. I haven't eaten yet and I'm hungry. Let's meet someplace that serves lunch and compare notes."

He'd already eaten, but wanted to talk. "How about the Come on In?" Some five miles south of the retirement home, it wouldn't take him long to get there. "See you soon."

It was a beautiful afternoon. Maybe he'd go riding later. He found Vi in a booth reading through the menu and slid into the banquette across from her. "Sure is a pretty day."

"A welcome change from dark, gloomy Gran."

A waitress stopped by. Vi ordered a burger and fries, and he asked for a pop.

She looked at him like he was crazy. "You're passing up a burger here?"

"Sadly, yes. Ross and I ate at Hastings. I'm coffeed out, too."

"Is he still doing a good job?"

"I'm happy with him so far. That meeting was a whole lot

better than sitting with Grandpop this morning. He was in a foul mood."

"Like I said, Gran was pretty down. She's still really mad at him. I wish they were less hardheaded."

"You can say that again. Malcom refuses to apologize."

"So Gran said. She even asked him to."

"This is what we wanted, for them to split up."

The food arrived, and Vi dug in. "This is so yummy. It really is the best burger around. You say you're not hungry, but the way you're staring at my food makes you look the opposite. Or did some of the sauce drip on me?" She frowned down at herself.

"No drips." Blake hadn't been looking at the burger, he'd been watching her face change when she bit into it. An eager, hungry expression that reminded him of their kisses the previous night. He wanted more, but she'd said she didn't. Before lunch ended, he intended to set her straight about who he was.

"Blake? I'm offering you some of my burger. It's way too big for me to finish."

She mesmerized him. Now, when they were talking about burgers and grandparents? What was the matter with him? He tore his gaze from her. "Hey, if you need help, I'm your guy."

Looking happier than she had a few seconds ago, she gave him half the burger and a generous portion of fries.

"That's too much," he said, "but I know you're depending on me to eat it."

She laughed, and the world brightened. "Back to Gran. She's not eating or sleeping much. From her slumped shoulders to her listlessness, unhappiness hangs all over her. I've never seen her this down. She even cried, which as far as I know she hasn't done since her husband died when I was a teenager." Vi chewed her lip. "Seeing her like that shredded my heart. She loves him, Blake, she told me so. Is Malcom as upset as she is?"

Blake recalled how miserable and defeated his grandpa had been. "He's a mess. He didn't use the L word, but he's suffering like a man whose world has tilted off its axis."

"Were you able to talk to him about that?"

"I tried. I suggested he apologize. You know him. He wasn't buying that. Let's hope what I said will sink in. I'll lay low for a day or so." Blake thought of something else. "One thing I didn't say but wish I had was that if he doesn't apologize and make things right, he'll lose her."

"He might need to hear that. I feel for both him and Gran, and I'm rethinking my opinion that they should break up. I don't mind if they're together as long as they slow down."

"I'm no fan of seeing Grandpop messed up like that, either. So, yeah, what you said."

She flirted with a smile. "Look at us, the flexibles."

For all his worry, Blake also brightened up. "It's unexpected, for sure."

"If only we knew what to do next."

"That could depend on what Caroline decides about her living quarters," Blake said.

"She's going to stay in her current unit. Her insurance check hasn't arrived yet, but I'm sure it will." Vi thought a minute. "If not, she'll have to move out. With the shortage of available units at other retirement facilities, she'll need an apartment for a while. My friend Carmie works at Port Simms Apartment Rentals. She's good at her job. If we need her to find something for Gran, she will."

"Good to have a backup plan. It'll be hard on them if they continue to live down the hall from each other."

"When I brought that up with Gran, she got huffy and pointed out that she knows how to be civil." Vi rolled her eyes. "They remind me of teenagers. On the plus side of her staying in her own unit, they won't need to rush into marriage if at all. Of course, they may not make up. But if Malcom apologizes to Gran, I know she'll take him back."

"He wants that, too, but he refuses to do what you and I think he should."

"At least they know how each other feels about money and keeping secrets. They both need to work on their communication skills."

Blake was glad she'd brought that up. "Like we do." She gave him a sideways look. "I'm thinking about last night."

The waitress stopped by with a dessert menu. Vi ordered pound cake with strawberry syrup, then continued. "I thought I was very clear—no more kisses."

"Yes, I heard you. But if you changed your mind, I wouldn't complain." Her eyes narrowed slightly and she pursed her lips in disapproval, and he stopped the teasing. "Some of what you said last night was confusing."

"The part about me sending you mixed messages—I thought about that and agree. I won't do it anymore. If I do, remind me."

It was good to know she was still willing to see him. "Okay. I meant the comment about me jumping from one woman to another. That's false, by the way, but we'll get to it later. You mentioned not wanting to be in that situation again. Someone must've done a real number on you."

She turned red, which was interesting. After the waitress

delivered the dessert and two forks, Vi cleared her throat. "I may as well tell you. I don't talk about this much, because it's old news and there isn't much to say. I'll keep it short."

She slid the cake plate between them and nodded at Blake to help himself but didn't pick up her own fork. Wanting to pay full attention to her, he ignored the cake as well.

"I wasn't popular in middle school or high school. People called me egghead, humorless, ugly—you name it," she went on.

Hard to believe. "No way," he said, frowning.

"It's true. I had a lot on my shoulders with taking care of my sister, cleaning house and staying on top of my homework, and I guess I was an easy person to make fun of."

She paused to sip water, and he imagined her as a young girl being saddled with responsibilities no kid ought to be carrying. He understood—he and especially his sister had been in a similar position.

Vi continued. "Things changed some when I went to college. My junior year, I met this guy, Devin. He worked on the grounds crew and wasn't a student. He was good-looking and sweet and built, and he was interested in me. Not one of the other prettier girls he could've chosen, me. I was surprised and flattered. We started seeing a lot of each other."

She paused and stabbed a bite of cake, but set the fork back down. "This is boring, huh?"

Wanting to hear the rest of the story, Blake shook his head. "Not at all. Please, go on."

"I fell for him hard. Things were good for a while, but then he changed. He borrowed money from me several times. I didn't have much to spare, but he was in a bind so I helped out." Her face clouded. "Cutting to the bottom line, I saw him kissing another girl. When I confronted him, he didn't apologize or try to defend himself, just headed for the door. I asked him to pay me back the money I loaned him. He didn't. After that, we avoided each other."

"So he borrows money and doesn't pay you back, and cheats on you, too?" Blake wanted to punch the guy. His hands curled into fists. "Sounds like a real ass."

"Times ten. He ripped my heart in half." She fiddled with a leftover fry. "Ever since, I've steered clear of getting involved with certain men."

"Such as?"

"I don't want to talk about that. Let's dig into the cake, okay?" She finally tasted what she'd forked. "This is delicious." After a moment, she added, "Anyway, last night triggered me."

The bite Blake had popped into his mouth lost its flavor. He was astounded. Did she think he was like that grounds crew jerk? "Comparing me with a liar and a cheat is insulting. In the first place, I'd never borrow money from you. Even if I did, I'd pay you right back. For the record, I don't cheat or flit from woman to woman. That's not who I am. Sure I date, but if we're not a good match and things don't work out after a few dates, we go our separate ways. I don't jump into bed with everyone I go out with, either." He met her gaze straight on so she'd know he meant it.

"Daisy thought you were a good match. She proposed to you."

Should've explained that earlier. "During the six or so weeks we dated, I never led her on. I kissed her goodnight the first few times we went out, but there was no chemistry. I was ready to call it quits and was going to tell her over dinner the same night she proposed in the parking lot. She wanted a man to take care of her and thought I fit the bill. It shocked me. We never talked about anything close to marriage, let alone dating each other exclusively. That's God's honest truth."

"I never imagined… Thanks for setting me straight."

The apology helped. "What happened to Devin?"

"I haven't kept track, but Carmie has. According to her, he lives here in town, has been divorced three times and works as a day laborer at some roofing company around here. I rarely think about him."

"But you did last night." Man, that bothered him.

She grimaced and nodded. "Now you know."

But he didn't, not really, and was deeply offended. Too much so to hang around with her and talk anymore. He stood, pulled his wallet out of his pocket and laid a couple of bills on the table. "Time for me to go."

* * *

VI DROVE HOME IN TURMOIL. It was obvious her story had upset Blake. She hadn't liked talking about it, but now it was out in the open. All of it except for the humiliating way she'd begged him to stay. Only Carmie knew about that. Vi wanted nothing more than to move on and think about other things. Like Rose coming home tonight and work Monday and Gran and Malcom, but her mind refused to cooperate.

She hated how she and Blake had parted ways, with him all tense and her feeling icky as she always did when she thought about the past. She was about halfway home when her Bluetooth signaled a call from Rose. "Hey, you," she said, happy to have something to take her mind off him. "What time do you get home tonight?"

"I just landed. Peter said he'd pick me up, but he's at a medical conference in San Francisco to give a talk about a surgery of some kind. He was supposed to arrive about the same time as me, but he texted seconds before my flight took off and let me know he won't be home till tomorrow night."

Vi couldn't tell if that was good or bad. "So you're going home to an empty house."

"Once I get there. It's a three-hour drive from SeaTac airport home, but at least I won't be the one driving. The person behind the wheel will make good money. After a week apart, I was looking forward to seeing Peter. Guess I shouldn't be surprised. This happens a lot at medical conferences."

Having never been to one, Vi had no idea about that kind of thing. "That's a shame."

"As you always used to say about stuff we couldn't change, it is what it is, right? I'll pour myself a glass of wine, take a nice, long soak in the tub and catch up on one of the shows I missed while I was gone."

"Were you sorry to leave the spa?"

"Yes, and I've already decided to go back again next year. Have you thought anymore about joining me?"

"Depends on my finances, but I'm thinking about it. If you have time tomorrow, Gran would love to see you. When I visited her this morning she was disappointed you weren't with me. I don't know why she thought that—she knew you were getting home around dinnertime tonight. Maybe because I dropped by unexpectedly."

"That's not like you, Vi. You always set up things like that in advance. When I call her later, we'll figure out what time works for her."

"I didn't want her to know I was coming because..." Vi

paused. There was so much to say, and she wasn't sure where to start. "I'd better update you first," she said as she neared the complex where she lived.

"More about the car accident? Is she hurt worse than you thought?"

"The opposite—she's healing nicely. This has to do with her and Malcom." Vi filled her in as she pulled into her garage and headed into the house. A wind had kicked up and clouds scuttled across the blue sky. She hoped it wouldn't rain.

"You didn't tell me about the fight at the restaurant," Rose said. "All that yelling must've been so embarrassing."

"I guess I forgot to mention that. It was uncomfortable, at least for Blake and me. Gran semi-apologized in passing, but as far as I know Malcom hasn't said a word about it."

"Poor Gran."

"Malcom, too. They're both suffering. Blake and I are changing our minds about them getting involved so quickly."

"That's twice you've mentioned him in the last few minutes. How is he?"

"Hello, Mr. T," Vi crooned as she entered the house and silently thanked him for saving her from talking about Blake. The tom meowed and twined himself around her ankles. "Sorry, it's too early for dinner."

"Give that sweet boy a smooch for me," Rose said. "My ride's here. Hey, why don't you come over around dinnertime?"

"I was about to invite you to the townhouse. We'll get take-out, okay?"

"All right. I'll show you my photos and tell you about my trip. And you can talk about Blake."

CHAPTER 15

Not long after he'd left the restaurant earlier and still seriously irritated that Vi had compared him to Devin, Blake needed to clear his head. A hard, fast ride should do the trick while tying in nicely with testing the Bad Boy 3 Bike, a new model hybrid that looked promising. If he liked it, he'd add it to the inventory at both bike stores. He changed into cycling togs and packed clean clothes and a waterproof jacket in the waterproof bike pack he always carried on rides, just in case.

After donning his helmet, he headed up the highway toward Port Simms Park and Lockleigh Trail. Before being repurposed into a trail, the Lockleigh had been a train track that circled the perimeter of the park and continued for nearly 40 miles. Perfect for the rigorous test he had in mind.

A while later, the wind picked up. No problem, he was used to pedaling uphill which was similar to riding against the wind. As always, he relished the effort needed to speed along. It was good to be outside, nodding to other bikers, noting the birds swooping in the wind and the signs of spring everywhere. Flowers, new grass, trees unfurling their leaves and fat with buds.

Savoring the freedom and joy of riding, he veered off the trail and segued onto another more rugged path farther away from home. The wind held a trace of moisture now, signaling an upcoming rain. He paused to pull the jacket from the pack and put it on. And realized he was only a mile or so from Vi's place.

What was he doing all the way out here?

Yes, he wanted to clear up the questions she'd put into his head and hadn't answered, but not a few short hours after they'd parted ways, especially when he stunk of sweat. Besides, he wasn't even sure she was home. On a Saturday afternoon she could be anywhere. She'd also made it clear that she appreciated a call first.

A raindrop splashed his cheek. He glanced up at the dark clouds rushing by as if being chased by more clouds behind them. This was going to be a doozy of a storm. A heavy downpour started, and he doubted the rain gear would keep him dry on the long ride home or that it was safe to ride in this weather.

Leaving him little choice where to go. Vi's it was.

He pedaled toward her townhouse.

THE WIND WAS fierce and rain pummeled the window. Vi thought about Rose. By now, she was either home or almost there. She texted her sister to let her know she was eager to see her, then sat down to scroll through the menus of various restaurants. Her mouth was starting to water when someone knocked at the door.

Could that be Rose? But no, Blake stood on the step wearing a bike helmet. She wondered about that. "Dropping by unannounced again? Don't make a habit of it," she scolded, but right now the poor guy needed shelter. "You're a wet mess." She gestured him inside.

He didn't move. "Is there a safe place to stash my bike?"

"In the garage. I'll open it." After shutting Mr. T in the broom closet to keep him from running outside, although in this weather she doubted he'd be tempted, she hurried into the garage and activated the garage door. Seconds after it slid upward, Blake wheeled the bike in. He wore bicycle shorts that hugged his narrow hips and reached to midthigh. The loose jeans he favored had only hinted at the powerful muscled legs exposed now. Wow. No doubt from the cycling he did.

"There's room in front of the garbage bin on that side," she said, pointing leftward. "The door on the opposite wall leads into the utility room. When you're finished, come through there."

"Will do. There's a change of clothes in my waterproof cycle bag. I'll bring that in with me. I sure hope the thing didn't leak."

"If it did, you can use the washer and dryer. Smart of you to pack a change of clothes." Had he planned to come over?

"I always bring extras for emergencies."

Then he hadn't expected to visit. Yet here he was. He unzipped the yellow jacket covering his torso and shrugged out of it. The tee underneath was wet. "I should've stopped and zipped up the Gore-Tex jacket sooner. Once I hang it someplace, it'll drip dry. I didn't expect a storm like this."

"It's coming down hard, the wind is crazy and you biked a long way from where you live."

"Thirty miles is nothing. I rode the trail for a while, too."

Odd that he'd come to the townhouse a few hours after walking out of the restaurant. She'd offended him. Maybe he'd intended to stop by and had come to talk more about it. But if that were true, wouldn't he have called to let her know? Once he was warm and dry, she'd find out. "There are hangers in the utility room."

He glanced down at himself. "I don't want to track mud into the house."

"Leave your shoes next to the mat here in the garage. I'll meet you in the utility room with a towel so you don't drip."

"I could use a shower."

The mud spatters attested to that. As soon as he entered the utility room with the cycle bag, she handed him a towel for his feet. Now that they were both in the house, she let Mr. T out. He stared at Blake, but didn't come any closer.

"I don't blame you, buddy," Blake said. "I'm a wet, stinky mess."

Vi agreed. He really needed that shower. She led him toward the bathroom, stopping to point out the adjacent linen closet. "There are more towels in there if you need them." Thankful she'd taken care of her wash earlier, she nodded at the empty laundry basket next to the cabinet. "Toss your things in that and put it outside the bathroom door. While you clean up, I'll start the washer. If it turns out your cycle bag also leaked, I'll get the clean clothes into the dryer right away."

"I wouldn't want to put you out."

"You're here, and I have time. It's no problem at all."

The stubborn set of his jaw reminded her of Malcom. "It is for me. I don't want you doing my laundry. After I clean up, I'll do it myself." He entered the bathroom and shut the door firmly.

All right, then. Moments later, she heard the shower start. Her cue to head back to the kitchen and finish looking through those dinner menus.

Instead, she stayed right where she was. Having him here in her house, standing under the shower spray in all his naked glory... Certain body parts got excited. She swallowed hard, then frowned. What had come over her?

Lusting for him was a bad idea. Dangerous. She marched herself back to the kitchen and wished he'd called first. If he had, she'd have told him not to come.

Or would she?

All she knew was she wanted him gone, preferably before Rose showed up. Yet here she was, pulling out the tin where she stored the coffee bin to brew a fresh pot.

Surely he wouldn't cycle all the way home in this weather. And they really did need to talk more. She hadn't meant to insult him during lunch and wanted to straighten out the misunderstanding. Now she was sending mixed messages to herself. She rolled her eyes ceilingward.

As she headed toward the bathroom again to find out if he was still in the shower, the sudden silence proved he wasn't. Like a fool, she stayed where she was, imagining him toweling dry and getting dressed. For way too long, as it turned out. She was about to dash back to the kitchen when the bathroom door opened.

Caught.

He flashed a smile. "Anxious to see me, are you?"

Too overconfident for his own good. Her cheeks felt hot. He was in jeans and nothing else, and water droplets from his hair dripped onto his broad shoulders. She was so awed by the site of his bare torso—the abs and biceps—that she was struck silent until she dragged her admiring gaze up to his face. "Don't flatter yourself. I'm standing here because I forgot to tell you where the hair dryer is," she ad-libbed, not a bad reason for lingering outside the door. "It's in the cabinet under the sink."

"Exactly where I found it. These jeans are fine, but the tee I packed is damp and definitely needs to go into the dryer. Do you happen to have a shirt I can borrow?"

As if anything of hers would fit him. She thought for a moment. "Not a top, but I do have a happy coat—a short, lightweight robe I wear in warm weather—that'll work. I'll bring it to you."

"I'd appreciate it. I'll try it on after I dry my hair."

When she returned from getting the robe from the bedroom closet, the hair dryer was on full blast. Super noisy, and she knocked several times before he opened the door. "Hard to hear with this thing going full blast," he said. "Still working on the hair." He stared at the bright pink flowers and the purple cotton sash laced through the belt loops on the happy coat and chuckled.

"You don't have to wear this. It's okay if you're bare-chested." She'd have to pretend she wasn't drooling, but guessed she'd be able to control herself.

"I'm not proud. Hand it over. I'll be out in a bit."

In the kitchen again, she ground the beans, started the coffeemaker, and grabbed two mugs from the cabinet.

Seconds later, wearing dry socks, he padded into the room with the laundry basket. The happy coat wasn't quite big enough to stretch fully across his chest. On her, the robe hung to midthigh; on him, it barely reached his hips. She tried to stifle a giggle and failed.

His eyebrows went up. "That bad?"

"Pretty awful. I should get a picture of you."

"Don't you dare," he said as she pulled her phone from her hip pocket and snapped several photos.

"Vi," he warned, a smile softening the tone. "Let me see."

He reached for her phone. She jerked it away. "Hand you my phone so you can delete these photos? I'll show you instead."

He set the laundry basket down and moved in close. Too close. Trying her best not to inhale his clean-soap smell, she showed him the pictures.

"What do I have to give you to make you delete them?"

All kinds of unwanted ideas filled her mind, most of them way too sexy to voice out loud. She stepped aside. "I promise not to share with anyone unless you misbehave." She giggled again. It felt good.

"Be on my best behavior—got it. The sooner my tee dries, the better. Do I need to know anything about operating the washer?"

"Laundry soap is on the top shelf. Otherwise, it's self-explanatory."

His hair was tangled and sticking up. He smoothed it with his palms, frowned, and smoothed again, for all the good that did. Wouldn't you know, the happy coat rose up another few inches, giving her a generous glimpse of his navel and flat belly. She glanced away and focused on that hair. She wanted to grab a comb, wet it and groom him. She wanted more than that. *Stop it.*

Anyway, she didn't share her comb and brush. "I'm about to make coffee if you want it."

"Go ahead. I'll join you when I get this stuff into the washer."

While he was gone, she considered texting Rose. Her sister needed to know he was here. At least when he was around, she wouldn't press Vi to talk about him. She postponed texting to pull a carton of half-and-half from the fridge and fill a small pitcher.

After the washer started, he padded into the kitchen. "Man, that coffee smells good."

"Help yourself. Half-and-half and sugar are on the counter."

For some reason, watching him fix his coffee was mesmerizing, especially with a decent swath of his chest exposed. Did he have to be so buff? Better stop ogling the man. She filled a mug for herself. "You should know that Rose is coming over soon. We're ordering takeout."

"Your sister's finally back. Got it. As soon as the laundry is done I'll call Falcon Ride Service and ask for a car that has room for my bike."

"Or you can have dinner with us." Had she really just invited him to join them? "Since it's pouring and you're here."

"Wouldn't want to impose." He glanced down at himself and snorted. "Guess I already am." They sat at the eating counter with their mugs. "I still have questions about what you told me earlier today."

"Considering the abrupt end of our conversation, I'm not surprised. When you left, you weren't happy."

"No, I wasn't. Your comment that what we did reminded you of the clown you got involved with really fried me. I've never been compared with anyone like that. You said you liked my kisses, but I guess you changed your mind."

"Believe me, I haven't," she replied, her lips tingling from the memory of his delicious mouth on hers. "That wasn't what set me off."

"Well, what did? Because sharing a few kisses is much different from borrowing money from you and cheating." His eyes blazed, and not in a good way, as they bored into hers.

A few tense seconds later, Vi sighed. "Apparently, my explanation wasn't as clear as I meant it to be because you're still mad."

"Ya think?" He paused and scratched a finger in his hair. "Huh."

"Huh, what?"

"I'm just now realizing what I'm really ticked about. Not you, the jerk who led you on and messed with your feelings."

He understood, a relief, and about the sweetest thing she'd ever heard. The more she got to know Blake, the more she liked him. She fought the urge to pull him close and admitted to herself that she was in worse trouble than she'd realized. It was time to pull back before she made a huge mistake. "I think we need to—" The chiming doorbell cut her off. "That's Rose."

Her sister blew in like a wind-whipped flower. The strands of hair across her face and pink cheeks only made her prettier. "Some homecoming this is. I didn't expect wind and rain, but it is mid-April." Her eyes widened and she cut herself off. "Hi," she said, staring at Blake in the happy coat. "I'm Rose."

"Blake." He nodded. "Believe me, I don't usually dress this way."

Her lips twitched. "Good to know. Nice to meet you. I've heard about you."

"Yeah?"

Vi felt his curious glance. Not wanting him to get the wrong idea, she jumped in. "I told Rose about Gran and Malcom inviting us to dinner that first night and about the accident."

His attention was on her sister. "What else did she tell you about me, Rose?"

The tom meowed and butted her sister, and she picked him up and cuddled him. "Hi, Mr. T," she cooed. "Did you miss me while I was away?" He wanted down and jumped out of her arms. "Vi's been close-mouthed. She hasn't told me much, at least not as much as I'd like. I was going to find out more about that tonight, but I didn't expect to see you."

"It was a surprise to me, too," Vi said, arching her eyebrows Blake's way. "You never said what brought you all the way over here."

He shrugged. "I was out riding in the area and got stuck in the downpour. End of story."

"But your house is on the other side of town. Why cycle all the way out here?" Vi asked.

"It wasn't something I consciously thought about. I wanted to test a new bike before I placed an order for the stores. Figured I'd ride part of the trail and then head back. Turns out, it's a terrific bike. I was enjoying myself too much to stop, so I kept going."

As explanations went, his fell short, but Vi didn't want to question him in front of Rose. "His wet clothes are in the wash and the spare shirt he brought got wet. It's in the dryer. That's why I invited him to stay for dinner, if that's okay with you."

"Of course. But be forewarned, Blake, I'm going to talk about my trip and share some photos."

"I don't mind. Vi mentioned you were at a spa."

Rose nodded. "In Cancun."

"My sister likes to go down there for the same thing."

"Oh? Which spa? Is she down there now?"

"I don't know the name, and no, she's on bedrest. She's carrying twins and her doctor doesn't want them to arrive for another three to four weeks."

"Boys, girls, or one of each?"

"One of each."

"That's exciting, but stuck in bed? Poor woman."

"It's rough, but she's doing all right. I thought sure you'd be with your husband tonight."

Rose's turn to shoot a questioning look Vi's way. "Plans change. He's at a medical convention till tomorrow night."

Vi watched closely as Blake interacted with her beautiful sister. Any man in his right mind would've flirted with her even if she was married. Not Blake. He was friendly but not overly so and basically behaved himself, when she'd thought sure he'd at least show her the sexy smile he sometimes flashed. "Hey, you guys," she said. "Let's figure out what we want for dinner. I checked several websites and want your input." She sent the links to their phones

It didn't take long to decide, and some minutes later she placed the order. "The food should be here in thirty minutes."

"That's fast. While we wait, I'll show you both some photos

I took." Rose yawned. "It's three hours later in Cancun. Is there any more coffee?"

Shortly before the food arrived, Blake's tee dried. During the meal, the three of them talked about the grandparents and Rose's plan to visit Caroline the following morning. "We're looking forward to seeing each other," she said and promised to keep them informed about whatever she found out.

By the time they finished the meal, the rain had shifted to a light drizzle. While Blake loaded the freshly washed clothes into the dryer, Vi saw her sister out.

"I like him, Vi. He seems like a great guy," she said in a voice too soft to carry. "Be nice to him."

CHAPTER 16

Vi's sister had hung around long enough for Blake to trade the ridiculous robe for his long-sleeve tee. He felt much better wearing it. It'd grown dark outside, and he ought to go home. While Vi stood in the threshold and watched as Rose headed for her car, he messaged Falcon and ordered a vehicle able to carry a bike.

"It'll be a good half hour before I get picked up," he said when Vi returned. That ought to give them enough time to finish the conversation Rose had interrupted earlier.

"Let's sit in the living room."

He chose a comfortable armchair. Vi plunked onto the couch across from him. "Your sister's good people," he said. "What did she whisper to you before she stepped outside?"

Looking like a cornered rabbit caught where it shouldn't be, she gave a closed-mouth smile, grabbed a throw pillow and hugged it. "It was about me, wasn't it?" he guessed.

She huffed out a breath. "Not everything is about you."

"Yeah, but this is." At her questioning face, he added, "Your expression gave you away."

Muttering something that sounded like "why me?" she glanced up as if irritated, but by the light tinge on her cheeks, that wasn't the issue. He eyed her. "Well?"

"All right, she mentioned you. Satisfied?"

"Not quite. I want to know what she said." She shook her head, reducing him to beg. "Please tell me, pretty please."

"Oh, all right. She thinks you're a great guy and told me to be nice to you."

"I like her even better now. Before she showed up, we were talking about what happened earlier today. You started to say something about us needing to do I don't know what because that's when she came in."

"Let me think back. I don't remember, except to say you're not at all like Devin. He's all brawn and little brain. You're smart and kind and caring."

Damn, he liked that. "Tell me why us kissing reminded you of him."

She sucked her bottom lip for a few moments. "He hurt me a lot, and I guess I'm worried about that."

"I don't go around breaking hearts."

"I doubt anyone sets out with that in mind, but at some point, it happens to us all."

The way she hugged herself, she must've been hurt a lot. "How many times have you had your heart broken?"

"Once."

In disbelief, he studied her. "Seriously?"

She nodded. "Devin was the first and only. I've learned to be careful. What about you?"

"I went steady a few times in high school, but those relationships never lasted. I had a breakup or two in college. Sure, each time it happened stung, but like almost everybody else, I survived. I'd been out of college for a while when I met Sammi. We thought we were madly in love. Then a few months before the wedding, we realized what we felt for each other was mostly about sex. We agreed getting married would be a mistake, called it off and went our separate ways.

"Splitting up was a mutual agreement but still hurt. For as long as I can remember, I'd pictured myself falling in love, getting married and having kids. Since the thing with Sammi, I've changed."

"How so?" Vi asked, toying with a confused frown.

A question he'd mulled over for a long time. "If an amicable breakup hurts, think how much worse it must be when a relationship ends in divorce or death. The emotional pain of either one must be almost impossible to bear. Not must be, is. If you'd lived with my mother after my dad died, you'd understand."

"With my parents, it was the opposite. They couldn't wait to get divorced."

"Different strokes, but bad outcomes either way."

"You're saying you don't want to fall in love?"

She seemed genuinely curious, and he thought a minute before answering. "I'm saying I'm not sure I ever have. There've been times when I thought I was in love and the feeling was mutual. The beginning always feels good, but not the end. And for me, it always ends. "I'm beginning to think I'm not capable of committing to the kind of relationship that lasts." He'd never admitted that to anyone, hadn't realized it himself until now.

She sucked on her bottom lip, fussed with her ponytail. "I think we all start out dreaming of love and marriage. I certainly did when Devin singled me out. I was twenty and guess I was looking for stability. Gran was living with us then, but money was tight, and Rose called a lot for advice. In other words, I was still responsible for my family. I needed someone to lift the burdens off my shoulders, and I was a late bloomer with nobody to give me good advice." She paused and shook her head. "My parents were and still are really messed up."

Blake could identify. "I hear that. My mother was a basket case for years. If it hadn't been for Grandpop and Grandmom, I don't know where I'd be."

"Thanks to the total lack of role models, I fell for the first guy who paid attention to me. Couldn't have been a worse choice. Looking back, I realize how lucky I was when he walked away. I can't imagine the nightmare my life would've been if we'd stayed together."

"I'm pretty sure that if Sammi and I had gotten married, we'd be divorced," Blake said.

"What's she doing now?"

"Last I heard, she's married with a couple of kids. I say good for her. You and I are older and wiser than we used to be. You understand me, and most of the time we get along great, even if we don't know each other well enough to think about a real relationship." As true as his words were, he felt as if he'd known her for years. "I like you, though, and I'm pretty sure the feeling is mutual."

He expected her to at least nod. When she didn't, he nudged her. "You like me, too, right?" he asked with a long, level look that ended when she glanced down.

"I guess so."

"Gee, thanks. Word, I won't kiss you again unless you want me to."

She finally met his gaze. "And I won't send mixed messages."

"Deal. In the meantime, I don't see why we can't hang out like we have been."

A corner of her mouth lifted. "Wouldn't that shock the grandparents."

"I picture us prying their jaws off the floor."

She hadn't verbally agreed to anything yet, which led him to the next bit of confusion. "There's something else I wonder about. During lunch this afternoon, you made a comment about steering clear of 'guys like me.' Then a few minutes ago you called me smart, kind and caring. Which of those is right?"

"You seriously want me to answer that?"

"If I didn't, I wouldn't have asked."

"Fine. Both are true."

Wondering at that, he scratched his head. "What's your definition of guys like me?"

Vi checked her watch and stood up. "Your ride should be here any minute now. You'd better get your bike and shoes and the rest of your stuff together."

Not ten seconds later, his phone beeped. "You're right—the driver's two minutes away." Which meant he wouldn't find out the rest of what he wanted to know tonight. Might never if she stayed so close-mouthed.

She accompanied him to the garage. There, he toed into his shoes, stowed the clean clothes and waterproof, now air dried jacket into the bike carrier before hooking it to his bike. The driver pulled up. "Talk soon," he told Vi and wheeled the bike out of the garage.

She stood there a minute before the garage door closed, leaving him more confused than ever.

* * *

FOR THE REST of the weekend, Vi stayed home and kept to herself. Rose phoned that the visit with Gran had been so-so due to Gran's melancholy and refusal to talk much. She simply didn't feel like it. So sad.

Her grandma wasn't the only one who needed solitude. Vi thought a lot about the previous day. Talking more with Blake last night had been both bad and good. Bad because she'd told him details about both herself and Devin she rarely spoke about. Good because she understood that he didn't consider himself capable of the kind of relationship she hoped to find someday.

It was a relief to know how he felt and would keep her from wasting her time wanting what he couldn't give. Even so, deep down and like it or not, she'd started to want that anyway.

She refused to let her feelings for him grow any deeper. After beating herself up for talking too much and for wanting what he couldn't give, she decided not to waste any more time thinking about him.

Foremost on her mind right now was work and how to make the best of a difficult situation. Chaos still reigned at the company. People continued to work long hours and grumble, and she worried that some might resign. She was almost there, too, battling with herself to suck it up, then thinking about working elsewhere.

Yet she loved working there, or had, and the low morale at

the company worried her. On Wednesday a full week and a half since the upheaval, she stopped by Todd's office to talk about it. Having been transferred to a new position as head of operations, he'd moved upstairs to join the other highest-level employees and no longer spent much time on the floor where most of the chaos reigned. He needed to know that everyone was frazzled and quickly burning out, herself included, and that she'd come up with a way to lower the tension level at least temporarily.

Todd seemed every bit as drained. "How are you holding up, Vi?"

"Doing my best. We both know it's only been a short while since everything changed. The future is an unknown and with a much smaller workforce, it's a zoo on the front lines. People are demoralized, and I worry some will quit. If that happened, the company would suffer more than it is now. I certainly don't want that to happen, and I know customers and clients would agree. I've come up with an idea that might help alleviate the pressure."

All ears, Todd leaned forward. "Oh?"

"What if we rehire some of the laid off employees? No promises they'll be able to keep their jobs, but as a way to help everyone for a little while. Can we do that?"

Her former boss regarded her. "I'm impressed, Vi. I barely have time to sleep, let alone problem solve. I'd have to run it by Mr. Iglesias. I can't promise anything—as you say, it's early days and he may want to wait and see how things settle before we consider making any more changes. Also, it could mean a giant headache for HR. But it's worth sharing with the big boss. It might help if you put a list together of people you recommend."

She hadn't thought about that. "When would you need it?"

"As soon as possible, but no later than Friday."

One more load on her already burdened shoulders. Nothing new there. She nodded. "I can do that."

Nibbling vending machine cheese and crackers for lunch, she set to work. In a perfect world, rehiring almost everyone would be ideal, but in reality, wasn't possible. She stayed at the office late Wednesday night compiling a list that included former employees with the most experience and strongest work ethic, plus several newer recruits with great potential. Finishing shortly after midnight, she delivered the list to Todd's office. He was gone, of course. She left it on his desk.

At home, poor Mr. T had eaten the remains of his breakfast long ago and was starving. He let her know with a series of demanding meows. "I'm sorry," she apologized. "I'll never, ever keep you waiting again."

She fell into bed and slept soundly until the alarm woke her the following morning.

As of Friday, she hadn't heard a word from Todd or the CEO. Both were as swamped as everyone else, and she guessed she wouldn't hear anything for a while.

It was what it was. Until something changed, she'd do her best to help others survive awhile longer.

CHAPTER 17

Late Friday morning, Blake phoned Grandpop. No answer, and he left a message. "It's Blake," he said, as if the man didn't know that. "It's been too long since I last visited you. I want to catch up. By now, your ribs and cheek should be healing. With the opening of the new store in less than two weeks, things are busy for me but on track. I've hired some good people and ordered bikes, cycling clothes and shoes, and other equipment bicycle enthusiasts need. Anyway, give me a call."

He wanted to ask about Caroline, but not in a voice message. Vi might know something. They hadn't been in touch since the previous Saturday night, and he figured she was as busy as him. Had life at the telecom company calmed down any? He wanted to know. Also, he missed talking to her. At almost noon, figuring this was as good a time as any to reach her, he phoned her.

Her cell rang several times and he figured she didn't want to talk to him. Ouch. He was about to leave a message when she picked up.

"Hi. It's crazy here," she said, the buzz of conversation he heard in the background attesting to that. "I can't talk long. Do you have news about Gran and Malcom?"

"No. I was hoping you did."

"She doesn't answer. I asked at the front desk. According to them, she's in the dining room every night. I guess she doesn't want to talk to me."

"I didn't think to check with the desk. They're both unhappy. When does she need the down payment for her unit?"

"Thanks for reminding me. Things here are so messed up, I haven't thought about the insurance check. I'm a bad grand-daughter."

If she'd forgotten that, she probably hadn't thought about him at all. Better than avoiding him. "What do you think about dropping in on them again sometime this weekend? Maybe we can do something to bring them together and talk through their differences."

"It's worth a try, but I wouldn't count on it. Hold on." The phone went silent. A few minutes later, she was back, this time breathless. "Mr. Iglesias, our new CEO, wants to see me."

"What's that about?"

"I don't know, and there's no time to explain. I'll call you back." She disconnected.

Calling him back, huh? If that wasn't a good sign... Smiling to himself, he headed out to pick up lunch.

* * *

AFTER A QUICK VISIT to the restroom to tidy her hair and freshen her lip gloss, Vi made her way to the second floor of the company where the big meeting room was located as well as the offices of Mr. Iglesias, Todd, and the telecom's other high-level executives. Not sure what to expect, she stopped at his secretary Peggy's desk. The same fifty-something secretary who'd worked for Alan Regan before he'd been sacked. "Hi, Peggy. I'm here to see Mr. Iglesias."

The woman greeted her warmly. "Yes, he mentioned that. I'll let him know you're here." A moment later, she hung up the phone. "He's waiting for you now."

The CEO's office was big and classy, with a view of the Pacific Ocean, as befitted his position. Like Todd and everyone else in the company, he looked exhausted. But he greeted her with a warm smile. "Sit down, Vi. Would you like coffee? I can ask Peggy to fix you a cup."

"No, thanks." She sat down and folded her hands on the desk.

"Todd shared your idea with me and passed on the list you compiled. I like what you came up with."

"Thank you. I'm worried about burnout and this will help ease some of the pressure."

"I agree. I ran your idea by HR and got the okay to temporarily rehire twenty of our previous employees. Depending on the state of our finances, we may be able to hire some of them back permanently."

Vi beamed at him. "That's great news. Everyone on the first floor will thank you."

"We're counting on it. We can't afford to lose any of our remaining employees. We also need to bring a few new upper management people on board."

"I wouldn't know who to recommend," she said.

"That's not why I called you here. Todd let me know you

were up for a raise and promotion before the bad news hit. I'm not able to restore your bonus or anyone else's at this time, but I would like to offer you a new position as executive sales manager for the company. As one of our vice presidents, you'll get a significant raise commensurate with your title and an office on this floor."

He wanted her for a job that far up the ladder? Vi could hardly believe her ears. Such exciting news and such a huge responsibility. She was both flattered and scared. "Thank you, Mr. Iglesias. I accept." She also needed time to figure out how to do the job. Not that she'd admit that.

"Excellent. When can you start?"

"How about next week?" she said, mentally calculating how to start off with a bang. It'd be nice to have a reference point. The previous manager in charge had been let go, but she may have left information behind. "Are there any notes on what was going on before we filed for bankruptcy?"

"Check with Peggy. Before I forget, you're going to need guidance, and Todd has offered to work with you. You can imagine how busy he is in operations, but he's available to meet this afternoon."

She could hardly believe her luck. Todd would be a big help. "That'd be wonderful. Should I keep the promotion to myself?"

"It won't be official until I make the announcement Monday and alert the press, but news is bound to get out. I don't mind if you want to tell people before then."

They talked a bit more, then Vi returned to the first floor. Make that, floated. She decided not to tell anyone at the company just yet—she wasn't sure how her friends and the remaining teammates would take the news. Family and friends outside the company were a different matter. It was lunchtime, and she headed to a nearby café to pick up food. As if she could eat. She bought a sandwich, a soda and a giant chocolate cookie to celebrate.

Still amazed and hardly daring to believe her luck, she itched to share the news with Gran, Rose, Carmie and Blake. She took her lunch to the car, where she'd have privacy, and then forgot about the food while she made calls.

The first was to Gran, who actually answered the phone. "I have exciting news," she said and shared it. "I won't get my bonus for a while yet, but my salary is going way up."

"That's wonderful, honey."

"Did you get the insurance check?"

"No, and I'm getting worried."

"Don't be. With my bigger salary, I should be able to take out a loan to cover you. Rose can help some, too." Depending on Peter.

"I hate to do that, Vi, but if I don't have the insurance money by next Wednesday, I may have to. As soon as I get it, I'll pay you both back."

"I'd rather you keep your money and let us do this as a way of thanking you for all you've done for us over the years, but I know you won't accept that. So yes, I'll consider it a loan. I'm sure Rose will, too."

"That's so reasonable. Why can't Malcom be like you girls?"

Ah, they were still at loggerheads. "I have to go, Gran. I'll talk to you later, okay?"

On the way home from work, she phoned Carmie. No answer. "I have news," she said via voicemail. "Get in touch when you can."

Then she phoned Rose. Her sister was thrilled for her. "What a shame you didn't get your bonus, too."

"I probably will in the future. Anyway, I'm very happy about the promotion. Gran will only take money from us as a loan and will pay us back when she gets the insurance check. If she gets it before the final date, she won't need to borrow at all."

"At least she agreed to let us help. I'll talk to Peter about that."

"Let me know what he says. Did Gran mention Malcom at all?"

"Only for a second. From the little she said, they haven't made up yet. That stubborn streak is creating big problems for her and always has."

"As we both know," Vi agreed. "Malcom is just as bad."

"I guess if I ever meet him, I'll see for myself. Their life is like a soap opera. When are you going to share your good news with Blake?"

"As soon as I get home."

"I'm sure he'll be happy for you. Promise me you'll let him in."

"What do you mean?"

"You tend to push people away. Don't do that with him. He's a keeper."

Vi hadn't expected that, but Rose was right. She tended to keep her distance, mostly with men. "Now you're playing the role of mother with me?"

"You did it for me for years, so why not? You could use some good advice."

Though Rose couldn't see Vi, she rolled her eyes. "I know you approve of Blake, but what makes you think he has any interest in me besides our mutual concerns about Gran and Malcom?" Other than a few kisses, as unforgettable as they were. "Right now, we're close because of the grandparents. Once that's settled, I doubt we'll feel the same way." At least Blake wouldn't.

"Oh, his interest goes further than that and vice versa. He looks at you like he cares. That night at your house I could almost feel the electricity between you two. Why not enjoy what you have while it lasts?"

"I want to, but like I said, I don't want to get hurt."

"I'd like to shake Devin until his teeth rattle."

"What good would that do?"

"It'd make me feel better. He should suffer for what he did to you."

"He doesn't care. Anyway, I'm over that and him."

"Prove it. Let your feelings for Blake run wild."

"Stop with the advice already. I don't need to hear that." No sense getting her hopes up when the man had admitted he didn't think he was capable of committing to anyone, especially long-term. Her feelings for him were already too strong, and she absolutely, positively didn't want to fall for him. "Let's drop the subject, okay? How's Peter?"

"He seems fine. He left early for the hospital. I don't know when he'll be home."

"He didn't tell you?"

"He said he'd be here for dinner, but you know how that goes. An emergency comes in and they're short-handed so he steps in. Such is the life of a much-in-demand surgeon." Rose was quiet a minute, then let out a sigh. "As busy as he is, I sometimes wonder if he's avoiding me."

Vi frowned. "He wouldn't do that. He loves you."

ANN ROTH

"Does he? Speak of the devil, he's calling now. Bye, and tell Blake hi from me."

Vi waited until after eating the pickings she found in the fridge and the giant cookie from lunch. Then she poured a glass of wine, toasted herself, and phoned Blake.

CHAPTER 18

After wolfing down a burger and sides at Come on In at the end of the Friday workday, Blake was restless. He'd made plans to visit his sister the following morning, but the evening yawned in front of him, and he wasn't in the mood to sit at home. Not after the busy week he'd had. He needed to go out and have fun.

A shame Vi hadn't phoned. Hours ago, she'd said she would. Not a word from her since, a disappointment but not unexpected. She'd gone cold on him and his questions the other night. Could he help wanting to know more about her? He knew stuff about her past, but for some reason she didn't want to get into the here and now, at least not with him.

The thing was, there'd been times before she'd agreed not to give him any more confusing messages, when her eyes, a pretty golden brown, had flashed longing, and he'd been sure she was interested in him.

Wishful thinking on his part, he decided, disappointed. He really liked her.

He was sitting in the parking lot, scrolling through the

movies playing tonight at the Crestwood, a funky movie house that showed oldies and foreign films, when she finally called him. Well, well. "Hey," he answered.

"Sorry I took so long to get back to you. It's been a crazy day."

Hearing from her boosted his spirits. She hadn't brushed him off after all. "Let me guess—you got that raise."

"How did you know?"

"When a CEO wants to meet with you, it's usually good news. Tell me."

"It's better than I ever imagined," she said, sounding happy. "You know how nutso work has been for all of us. Things have been so bad, I worried about burnout. Not just my own, everyone's. I came up with a simple way to help with that and ran it by Todd, my former boss. He liked the idea and passed it along to Mr. Iglesias."

"You must've impressed him."

"Enough that he bumped me up big-time in the chain of command. You're talking to the sales management executive and vice president. Eee!" she squealed. "Hope that didn't hurt your ears."

"Are you kidding?" He grinned. "I love that enthusiasm. Great news like yours should be celebrated. Let's go out and do it up right." During her long pause, his elation dimmed. "You probably have plans."

"Actually, I don't. No one at work knows about this yet and won't until Monday. But yes, I'm in the mood to celebrate. What do you have in mind?"

Heck if he knew, although he had a few thoughts. "Have you eaten?"

"Yes, but nothing celebratory."

"We'll have to rectify that in the near future. This is spur of the moment, but are you a fan of blues music? This is blues night at the Highway Club. Tony Jenkins and the Magic Fingers is playing."

"I like that kind of music, but I don't know the band."

"They're great musicians."

"Now I'm excited. I don't even know where the club is."

"About seven or so miles from Come on In. I'm just leaving there."

"Why didn't I think of that for dinner? It would've been so much better than a hot dog and can of baked beans. What's the dress code?"

"Jeans, sweats, whatever feels comfortable."

"I'm not wearing sweats. What about you?"

"Still in my standard work clothes—jeans, sneakers, and a comfy shirt."

"Funny, that's exactly what I changed into when I got home. But I think I'll go a little less casual."

"And here I thought we'd show up looking like twins."

"Because we look so much alike," she deadpanned, and he pictured a teasing smile on her face. "What time does the music start?"

Blake checked his watch. "Soon. I'll pick you up."

"Why would you do that when you're so close to the venue? Coming all the way to my house and back will take too long. I'll drive myself and meet you there."

"Hey, we're celebrating you."

"Which we will, once we see each other."

She sounded firm about that, and he let it go. "Your choice. I'll get the tickets and a table. See you soon."

* * *

FROM THE OUTSIDE, the Highway Club was pretty much as Vi had pictured it. A one-story building with ample parking and lots of vehicles in the slots. Inside was a surprise. Homey wood-paneled walls decorated with photos of musicians, a few of them well-known celebrities and others she didn't recognize. A decent-size stage front and center. To one side, a bar with a big whiteboard listing food and drinks. Tables, both big and small, filled most of the large space.

Recorded music played while the crowd ate, chatted and sipped drinks. Relieved to have made it before the band started, she paused just inside the door, shrugged out of her fitted, lightweight jacket and scanned the area for Blake. There he was, standing halfway between where she was and the stage. Tall, broad-shouldered and gorgeous, his cotton polo shirt showcasing his hard chest and abs. The mere sight filled her with longings that she quickly pushed away.

Uh-uh, no. Not tonight. She'd come to celebrate her promotion with him, period. She started toward him, making her way around tables. It wasn't hard to know when he caught sight of her. He waved and flashed the grin that lit up his whole face. Talk about giving her heart palpitations. Clamping down the impulse to rush toward him, she slowed her pace and pulled herself together.

"You got a great table," she said as she joined him.

"I lucked out." His gaze roved over her. "I like that rainbow-colored skirt with the—what do you call the layers?"

"A tiered skirt. It's not something I wear at work, but it seems right for a club."

"Good choice. Can I get you something to eat or drink? Champagne to toast your success?"

"Slow down there. I haven't even started the job. I'm going to have a ginormous learning curve, and I may not be a success for a while, so no champagne yet. But a Cosmo sounds good. What about you?"

"Beer." He raised his hand and signaled a server. "Any objection to mixed nuts?"

"Since I'm a bit of a mixed nut myself, none at all."

He chuckled. "You're fun tonight."

"I feel fun. You're in a good mood yourself."

"Do you want anything else? Cookies, ice cream, something like that?"

"I confess to eating a cookie earlier, but maybe later."

The server, a harried-looking woman who Vi guessed was in her early forties, took their orders and offered Blake a flirty smile before she hurried off.

Vi shook her head. "I can't believe she flirted with you."

"She smiled, that's all."

"At you and only you."

His eyes twinkled. "Are you jealous?"

"Did you really say that? I merely made an observation."

"FYI, while she was looking at me, I was looking at you. I like that top."

She'd changed into a soft-yellow silk pullover blouse with a V neck and three-quarter sleeves. "Thanks. I wore it because spring is here and it goes well with the skirt. When does the live music start?"

"Another twenty minutes or so. Who's going to help you with that learning curve?"

"My former boss, Todd. He's been moved out of sales but

171

has offered to answer questions and guide me. He'll be a great mentor."

"A mentor is a good thing. Grandpop was mine. Without his help, I don't know if I'd have opened a business of my own." He paused. "I tried to reach him again tonight. No luck. That's three nights in a row. I was worried and per your suggestion, contacted the front desk to find out if he's taking meals in his unit or in the dining room. According to them, a mixture of both."

"So we know he's progressing—physically, at least. I got through to Gran. I told her about my promotion and raise and asked about the insurance check—thanks again for reminding me about that. She still doesn't have it and worries it won't come in time. She needs it by next Wednesday. I told her if it hasn't come by then, I'll take out a loan. Thanks to my new salary, borrowing won't be a problem. We agreed she'll pay me back when the check arrives, because that's what she wants. She made a comment along the lines of why couldn't Malcom be reasonable like me. I guess they're still at odds."

They shook their heads at each other and shrugged. When the server delivered the nuts and drinks, Blake made a point of focusing totally on Vi, which made her uncomfortable. "Stop staring at me," she said.

"I wanted to show the waitress where my interest lies. Look—the band is here."

The musicians broke into a toe-tapping song that had Vi swaying in her seat. "They're really good."

"Speak up—can't hear you," Blake said loud enough for her to hear. "It's too noisy."

Vi raised her voice. "I said they're good."

Frowning, he moved his chair closer to hers and pointed to his ear. "Say again?"

The last thing she wanted was to have him close enough to feel the heat from his body. She cupped her hand around his ear. He smelled good—clean and fresh and Blake—and she almost drooled. "I like the band," she said, then shifted away from him.

People were flocking to the dance floor. "This music is too good to waste sitting here," he said. "Let's go."

She hadn't danced in ages and hadn't expected to, but why not? After all, this was a celebration. She pushed her chair back, he reached out a hand and helped her up, and they made their way through a tangle of people getting their groove on right there beside their tables. At last, they entered the packed dance floor. Dancing together was fun. She couldn't stop smiling. Blake seemed to be having a good time, too. Now and then, they joined others and danced as a group. The lack of space meant occasional jostling with people and a ton of laughter.

Sometime later, hot and spent, she was ready for a break. "I need to use the ladies' room. I'll meet you at the table."

"Are you as thirsty as I am?" Blake said. "I feel for the servers. They're running all over the place. While you do your thing, I'll get us a couple of waters and fresh drinks at the bar. I don't see much of a line there."

In the bathroom, Vi splashed water on her hot face, freshened her lip gloss, and combed her hair. It sure needed combing. Tonight with Blake was so much fun, and she smiled as she left the bathroom.

As she looked for him at the bar, a heavyset male bumped

into her. With a shock, she realized she was face-to-face with Devin.

"Hey, Vi," he drawled with a cocky grin. "Never figured I'd run in to you in Port Simms. Lookin' good."

He sure didn't. Besides a double chin, he'd aged quite a bit more than most guys his age. His hair was short but rumpled, and his cologne was so strong she wanted to gag. He looked her up and down with an intrusive, lecherous gaze. He was swaying a little, too. Drunk, she realized.

"Excuse me," she said and attempted to move around him.

"Wait." He reached out and grasped her arm with meaty fingers. "What are you doing here tonight?"

"Please, let go of me."

Ignoring her words, he held on. "Aw, c'mon. We haven't seen each other in years. Don't you want to catch up?"

She narrowed her eyes. "Get your filthy hands off me now."

CHAPTER 19

Blake eyeballed the scene unfolding near the women's bathroom. Who in hell was holding onto Vi like he never wanted to let go? "I'll pick up the drinks in a minute," he told the bartender. He strode toward her in time to hear her order the harasser away.

The man held up both his hands. "Cool down, Vi. I—"

"Back off," Blake threatened, his fists primed to throw a punch.

"Blake," Vi said with obvious relief. "I'm so glad to see you."

The man, obviously drunk, squinted at him. "Who're you?"

The answer fell out of Blake's mouth without missing a beat. "Vi and I are together." Tonight, they were. He put a protective arm around her. She didn't seem to mind, sank against him willingly.

The man's jaw dropped. Not counting reeling some, he didn't budge. "You've had too much to drink, buddy. Get lost, or I'll call security," Blake warned.

"All right, all right, I'm going. See you around, Vi."

"Not if I can help it," she muttered when he was out of earshot. "Thank you, Blake."

He felt her tremble and tightened his arm around her. "Wish I'd come sooner. Who was that jerk?"

"Believe it or not, Devin."

Oh, man. "The cretin from the grounds crew."

"Unfortunately. I was coming out of the bathroom and he bumped into me. He looked at me like I was a piece of meat."

She shuddered, and Blake wanted to deck the guy. "You okay? I can go after him."

"He's not worth it. I can't believe how bad he looks. I'm doubly grateful I haven't seen him since college. How did you know he—"

"While I waited at the bar for our drinks, I glanced toward the restrooms and there you were. With him." The thought of those hands on her...

"Don't squeeze me so hard."

He realized his arm had tightened too much and relaxed. "Sorry about that. Do you want to go home?"

"No, but I don't want to be here, either."

He didn't blame her. "Bastard really shook you up."

"Yes. I don't want to run into him again."

Blake seconded that. "I left our drinks at the bar. Come with me while I let the bartender know we've changed our minds. I want to alert him about Devin, too."

When Blake told the man, he nodded. "As soon as I saw what he was doing, I notified security. You okay, miss?"

"Yes, thanks," Vi said, but Blake knew how shaken she was. "He's too drunk to be driving."

"We're on it."

The band came back and started a new set. As toetappingly good as the music was, he wanted to get her out of there. "Drunkenness is no excuse for what he did," he said close to her ear as they headed toward the table to get her jacket. She'd left her hair loose, and flyaway strands teased his cheek.

"You're more upset than I am."

"Probably. I'm also proud of you. You held your own. If Devin hadn't let go of you, I figured you'd kick his shin."

"I never even thought of that. I was too stunned and scared."

"Could've fooled me."

"Thanks, but you're the man who got rid of him. My hero." She gave him a weak but grateful smile.

"I did what any decent man would. Where do you want to go?" he asked as they made their way to the exit.

"I have no idea except that I don't want to be around other people right now."

Fine with him. He wanted to be alone with her, hold her and make her feel better. No fooling around—she'd been through enough for one night. Besides, she'd made it clear she didn't want that. "It's a warm night and there's a full moon. My deck overlooks the ocean. Of course, we can't see the water, but the reflection of the moon on it should be fantastic. You'll love it. I'll behave myself, I promise." He caught his breath.

"I guess that'll do," she said, and he could breathe again. "I'll follow you to your house."

She was still upset, and he wanted her in the car with him. "I'll drive, then drop you back here at the parking lot when you're ready to go home."

"Why are you offering, when I'm perfectly able to drive?"

"I want to, okay?"

"How can I argue with that?"

* * *

As Blake navigated through the darkness, Vi attempted to calm down. But the adrenaline still flooding through her kept her from relaxing. She reviewed what'd happened at the Highway Club. Seeing Devin planted in front of her and grasping her arm in his too-warm grip... Ugh. She shuddered all over again.

What if Blake hadn't seen what was happening? Would security have come as quickly?

The important thing was he'd noticed and acted. She'd started out the evening intending to keep her distance from him. But they'd had such a good time dancing that she'd begun to feel differently. Those feelings had only grown stronger after what'd happened. He was a good man, and he cared about her. He'd told Devin they were together. Did he mean that, or were they mere words uttered to get rid of the drunken menace?

"You're awful quiet," Blake commented at a red light. "Sure you're okay?"

"Getting there. You were wonderful tonight."

"Wish I'd seen what was happening sooner."

"Don't worry about that. What matters is you were there."

"I guess."

He started to reach for her, then stopped himself. Wanting his reassuring touch, she caught hold of his hand. "Thank you."

"You're welcome."

He gave her fingers a gentle squeeze. Despite the darkness outside, she was able to see the gleam of warmth and caring in his eyes. The light turned green and she sat back. "Hey, Blake, do you think we could stop at Melissa Ann's? We're not far from the bakery now, and they don't close for another fifteen minutes."

"That's a great idea."

Moments later, he parked. "Feel like coming in, or should I surprise you?"

For some reason, she wanted to stay close to him. "I'll come in with you."

There were several customers in the store. She reached for his hand again. His warm fingers wrapped around hers, and he almost smiled. While they selected their treats and he paid, she realized that something inside her had changed tonight. Maybe it was time she stopped holding herself back from doing what she really wanted, to be held and kissed and adored even for a short period of time. To let feelings run wild as Rose had suggested.

A scary thought. *Don't do it*, a little voice in her mind urged. *I don't expect anything serious to come of it, so I won't get hurt*, she answered back. Talking to herself and answering— that was a new one.

She wanted what she wanted—him—and that was that.

Moments later, treats in hand and back in the car, Blake drove on. "Suddenly, you seem different," he said after another long silence.

"What happened tonight gave me the willies."

"I don't blame you. But your whole vibe has changed."

Wondering at that, she glanced his way. "How so?"

He was quiet a moment, thinking, she guessed. "I can't describe it. Less tense, like you're calming down."

The man had no idea. "I'm better," she said and wanted to show him exactly what had changed.

Slowing, he signaled. "We're almost there."

"That didn't take long." Decorative street lights illuminated big lots and houses that were lit up inside. "You live in an upscale neighborhood. Maybe it's the lights, but being here gives me a good feeling."

"Funny, that's how I felt when the real estate agent showed me the house."

He pulled into a driveway but stopped short of the garage. She wondered what he had packed in there. Oh, please, don't let him be a packrat.

"The shed out back where I kept my bikes and equipment was in bad shape," he said, almost as if something in her expression gave her thoughts away. "The contractor demolished it and hauled out the mess. He's getting ready to build me a new one. Until then, I'm keeping everything in there."

Then not a packrat. From what he said, anyway. She hadn't seen the inside of his house. A two story that looked to be a decent size. "Your house is much bigger than mine."

"Three bedrooms isn't that big. I bought it because I wanted a place that was mine, plus I liked what I saw."

"Stability. I know that feeling."

He nodded. "I'll give you a quick tour, then we'll sit out on the deck with our treats and wine or pop. Your choice."

"Wine sounds good."

She enjoyed seeing the house. On the main floor, a living room about twice the size of hers with a gas fireplace, comfy-looking chairs and a sofa. Also a dining room and a kitchen big enough for a table, plus a full bath and a bedroom he used as a home office. Upstairs, another full bath and the additional two bedrooms. The smaller of the two for company and the other where he slept. A glance around showed no signs of clutter. He wasn't a packrat or a messy person. Check and check.

But the deck out back was her favorite. Soft outdoor lighting illuminated a fenced yard. Beyond that, darkness. The house was close enough to the ocean to smell it, and she could hear the rush of the waves. "I love being out here," she said from her comfortable lounge chair. Blake sat in its twin, a wood patio table between them. "You were right about the moon. Its reflection on the water is so pretty." Also romantic.

"I knew you'd like it. You should see the view in daylight."

"Maybe you'll show it to me someday," she said, trying not to want that too much. "I'm ready for my treat." The bakery box was on the table. She opened it and salivated at the aroma of the chocolate eclairs.

They set their treats on napkins, and Blake poured the wine.

While they enjoyed the desserts, she heard a hooting sound. "Is that an owl?"

"Yep. They like the tall evergreens in the area. So do the eagles."

"Wow." Wishing she could sit next to Blake and cuddle up, she glanced longingly at the glider swing at the side of the deck.

"Would you rather sit there?"

She nodded. "I've never been in a swing like that. It looks fun."

"It can be. Mind if I join you?"

"Not at all." Pushing the seat back and forth with her foot was relaxing. "Know what?" she said. "I'm not stressed out anymore. The moon is so bright tonight, we don't need the outdoor lights."

"I'll turn them off."

He started to stand. "I'll do it," she said, rising and flicking the switch. "I can still see you clearly." She frowned at him. "This time, you're the one with something on your face— chocolate."

"Oh? Where?"

"I'll show you." She slid closer to him, leaned up and planted a kiss on the corner of his mouth. "Right there." Feeling both daring and awkward, she licked it off. "You're good now."

He went very still. "What are you doing, Vi?"

She smiled at him. "I've decided kisses are okay."

"You sure about that? This isn't a way to blot out what happened earlier?"

"I don't think so, but let me kiss you again to make sure." She gave him a teaser kiss, which wasn't nearly enough. "Nope, it's not about that at all. It's about you and me and nothing else." She pulled him down for more.

He groaned softly and wrapped his arms around her. "I've been wanting to hold you since we left the Highway Club."

"Me, too. Now be quiet and kiss me again."

This time was more intense. He tasted of chocolate and wine. Ambrosial.

"I can't get enough of your mouth," he murmured.

"Really?"

His reply came in warm, ardent kisses that involved tongues and squirming on her part. The world shrank down to her and him. She lost herself in sensation. His strong arms around her, the heat from his body, the smell of him. Before she knew it, she was sitting on his lap, enjoying his every move.

He nuzzled the sweet spot beneath her ears, kissed the skin exposed on her V neck top. She grew damp between her legs. Hungry for him, she wanted his hands and mouth on her. Everywhere. She angled back and thrust out her breasts.

His warm hand slid inside the V and down the top edges of her bra. Fingers on either side of her nipple teased and stroked, making her wild. One nipple, then the other. Craving more, she squirmed and pushed her breasts harder against his hands.

"Like that, do you?"

"Yes." She was about to take off her top when he inched back for a few disappointing moments. Then, thank you, God, he slid his hand under her skirt, up her thigh... Certain female body parts got all excited.

"Your legs are gorgeous."

The compliment barely registered—she was too focused on other things. *Feel free to slide that hand on up*, she silently urged, shifting restlessly on his lap. He was aroused. That made two of them.

Suddenly he broke away. He was breathing as hard as she was. "If kisses are all you're ready for, we should've stopped a while ago."

She wanted to stay exactly where she was and let nature take its course, but he was right. Pulling back was a wise choice. She climbed off his lap and scooted toward the far edge of the glider. "Maybe it's time for you to take me to my car."

On the drive back, they didn't talk much, and the events of the evening played through her mind. Dancing, Devin, kisses and more on the glider.

"Hey, Vi?" Blake said as he pulled up beside her car.

"Hmm?"

"I thought you stayed away from guys like me, whatever that is."

"It doesn't matter anymore," she said and meant it. Smart or not, she'd moved beyond caution. "Not counting what happened shortly before we left the Highway Club, I had a great time tonight. Thanks for celebrating with me."

She exited the car, and he followed suit. "What are you doing?" she asked and unlocked the Hyundai.

"I need a goodnight kiss, and we're not doing that in the car."

He lifted her up and hugged her close. Chest to chest, hip to hip. Delicious. "Mmm," she said, pressing closer. When he set her down, letting go of him wasn't easy. With reluctance, she stepped away. "Good night, Blake."

"Night." He stayed where he was until she buckled in and started the car.

CHAPTER 20

Vi was asleep and dreaming about steamy things featuring Blake and herself when the opening bars of "old time rock & roll" on her cell woke her up. She'd been so dazed from the night before that she'd forgotten to put the phone in do-not-disturb mode. And this was Saturday, a day to sleep in, "Hello?" she mumbled, propping her head up on her pillow.

"Hey, it's Carmie. Sorry if I woke you," she said, sounding anything but apologetic.

Vi checked the time. Barely seven a.m. "I didn't get to bed till late. What's up?"

"You left a message yesterday for me to phone you back. I want to know all about your news, but first I have a juicy announcement of my own." Without a pause for comment, she went on. "If you remember, Chris took me to Sweet Sue's last night. He finally did it, Vi—proposed. I'm officially engaged!!"

Fully alert now, she sat up. "Congratulations!" As thrilled as she was for her friend, she was also envious. Her thoughts went straight to Blake. They hadn't known each other long enough for anything close to serious. Besides, he wasn't a long-term relationship type guy. "Have you set a date?"

"Not yet, but we're thinking sometime early next year. That gives us time to plan. I do have a ring, though," she said, sounding very happy.

"Send me a photo?"

"I could, but I'd rather show you in person. Let's meet for coffee in an hour. Does that give you enough time? I have to be at work by ten."

"I'm already up, so sure."

"Quick question before we disconnect. Do you think your grandma wants to rent a place? You never said."

Vi hadn't given Gran a thought last night. Another guilt pang. She needed to touch base with her today. "I don't think so. I'll save my news till I see you. I have a strong craving for a fresh-baked cinnamon roll. Let's meet at Melissa Ann's Bakery."

"I'm so in. See you in an hour."

The bakery was packed with early risers. The aromas of good coffee, fresh-baked muffins, and other breakfast pastries made Vi's mouth water.

She spotted Carmie at a table. Looking perky for eight o'clock on a Saturday morning, her friend flashed a huge smile. "I got here early enough to get us a table," she said. "I'm starving. Let's hang our jackets on the chairbacks and get our coffee and cinnamon rolls. Oh, and check this out." She held out her left hand, where a sparkly diamond glittered on her ring finger. "It's two carats, and I absolutely love it."

Again, the prick of envy. "It's a beauty," Vi agreed.

"I don't know how Chris chose exactly what I dreamed of,

but he nailed it. He had it sized, too. Sneaky man borrowed a ring from my jewelry box."

Carmie continued to chatter on until a person at the counter called their names. They collected the orders and soon returned to the table. "Enough about me," she said. "What's your news? You sounded happy when you left the message, so it must be something good."

Eager to share everything, Vi started with the promotion. "Mr. Iglesias will announce it to the staff on Monday. It's going out on media then, too. That's when I'll tell the people I work with."

"The big guns are sharing the news with the media? I'm impressed, but then it's a well-known company and a big job, and you *are* a vice president. Congrats! If I'd known, I'd have treated this morning. I'll make it up to you another time. I hope you're planning to celebrate."

"I already did last night."

"Wonderful. Who with?"

"Blake."

"You told him?"

"Also Gran and Rose. He's been really supportive and deserved to know." He made her feel good about herself. "He was super happy for me and offered to take me to a live concert at the Highway Club. Tony Jenkins and the Magic Fingers played."

"Chris and I went there once, for comedy night. It's a cool place. I don't believe I've heard of that band."

"I hadn't, either. They're a blues group and amazing. When they started playing, we couldn't sit still. Most everyone got up and danced."

"Sounds like a really good time. Wait, you and Blake

danced? I don't think you've done that in forever, not in public."

"I know. We had so much fun. He's a pretty decent dancer. We didn't stop till the band took a break. Then…" Vi broke off. She didn't want to talk about Devin but ought to tell her bestie. "Something bad happened." Lowering her voice, she shared the icky details, ending with Blake coming to the rescue.

"That's horrible," Carmie said with a sympathetic look. "Thank goodness for Blake, your knight in shining armor."

"He truly was. I was scared and upset, and he calmed me down. The bartender saw what happened and called security. By then, Devin had disappeared. I hope they found him before he got into his car. He was in no shape to drive. I didn't want to stay at the club or go home and be alone, either, so we left and went to Blake's house."

"Oh, really. Care to elaborate?"

"Back up, first we stopped right here and picked up eclairs. They were freshly baked, too."

"Yum. Chocolate always helps. I wish they had fresh eclairs ready now to box up for later. I'm more interested in what happened at Blake's." Eyebrows raised, Carmie leaned forward in anticipation.

"We didn't talk much on the drive, silence I needed, and by the time we pulled into the driveway I felt much better. He lives in an upscale neighborhood on the east side of town and has a really nice house. We sat on his deck, which happens to face the ocean, and looked at the full moon reflecting on the water. I've seen that before, but not on a private deck, eating treats, sipping wine and talking to Blake. I felt normal again and at peace."

"Sounds romantic. And?"

"A few nights ago, I'd told him I didn't want to get physical."

"A few nights ago when?"

"The evening it rained hard and the wind was crazy. He was out cycling, got caught in it, and needed a place to dry off. He happened to be near the townhouse, a surprise to me, and knocked at my door. He stayed for a while."

"And you're just now mentioning this? Never mind—tell me about last night and not getting physical."

"He listened and didn't lay a finger on me."

"That's it?" Carmie looked disappointed.

"Not by a long shot," Vi said and lowered her voice again. "I changed my mind. We kissed. A lot. Actually, a little more than kissing, but nothing too exciting." Just enough to turn her insides into a hot mess of longing. At the same time, she was nervous. Her feelings for him had expanded to the point where she was already in too deep.

"I know that uncomfortable look. What are you leaving out?"

"I'm on the verge of falling for him," Vi admitted, "and it scares me."

"Why?"

"You know the answer to that. I don't want to get hurt."

"Maybe you won't."

"Believe me, I will. A gorgeous guy like Blake is bound to meet someone prettier and less dull than me."

Carmie hooted in disbelief. "Are you hearing yourself? When it comes to work, you're one of the most confident women I know. I admire you so much for that. But in matters of the heart, that confidence is missing."

"I heard the same thing from Rose."

"And high time you changed your opinion. It's been a long time since you fell for someone. Blake isn't like Devin. I know that and I haven't even met him. But if worrying keeps you up at night, maybe you should slow down on the physical thing until you're more comfortable with him."

"I don't know if I can," Vi admitted in a small voice. Or if she wanted to. "I'd like to boost my self-confidence, but how?"

"That won't happen overnight, but with persistence, you can build it up a little at a time. Start by looking in the mirror and loving what everyone but you sees—beauty and warmth and a spirit that shines. Repeat those words out loud with heartfelt sincerity whenever you see your reflection or any time you think about it. Call it your mantra. Always stand tall with your head high. Emulating self-confidence helps you look and feel that way."

"How do you know all that?" Vi asked.

"From a podcast I listen to. I repeat positive, loving words to myself every morning before I leave for work and again before bed." Carmie glanced at her smart watch. "Speaking of work, I'd better go or I'll be late. Love you, girl. Whatever you do and whatever happens, I'm here for you."

BLAKE HADN'T SEEN his sister in too long. Saturday morning, he hopped on his bike and cycled to her place. An easy ride, as she lived only a few miles away. This was another beautiful day. The sun was shining, birds chirped and sang, and the scent of flowers perfumed the air. For no reason, everything reminded him of Vi. Since he'd dropped her at her car the previous evening, she'd been on his mind constantly.

But then lately, that was a given. So much about last night had surprised him. Her about-face and kissing him with so much hunger and enthusiasm had been off-the-charts hot. He wanted more than kisses. He really liked her. Trouble was, he wasn't sure if his feelings were more about lust than anything else. Like with Sammi. At least Vi knew the truth about him and his doubts about committing.

He didn't want to hurt her.

No reason to tell Whitney any of that. Nothing to share right now, anyway. He wanted to talk about her and how she was feeling. Also about Grandpop.

Some minutes later, he coasted into the driveway. Her husband James was outside weeding and gardening. As soon as he saw Blake, he laid his tools down and straightened. "Hey," he greeted, grinning as Blake braked to a stop and hopped off the bike.

"Good to see you, man." Blake clapped him on the shoulder. They were about the same height, and he liked the guy.

"Cool bike," James said, studying the thing. "What is it?"

"It's called a Bad Boy 3, a new hybrid, which means it can tackle both on-road and off-road riding. I test-rode it the other day and like it so much I'm keeping it. Why don't you try it out."

"Okay, but just for a few minutes." James cycled down the driveway, rode a block or two, then circled back. "Sweet bike. I covet it."

"If you decide you want one, let me know. Shouldn't take more than a few days to get it."

"Better hold off. I don't know when I'll find the time to

ride, not with Whitney stuck in bed and the twins coming soon."

A software analyst, he worked at home. "She probably wouldn't mind," Blake said.

"I know for a fact she'd enjoy the space, but what if something happened and I wasn't there? She's looking forward to visiting with you."

"I want to see her, too." Blake pulled a bag from the bike carrier. "A little something for her. If you want to go out while I'm here..."

"I think I will. I need to pick up a few things for the yard."

Blake headed inside the house, which had plenty of space for twins. He found his sister on the sofa in the living room, propped up on pillows and reading a paperback.

"Hi." She set the book aside and gave him a warm smile.

"Hey. Look at you, about to burst."

"That's how I feel. Depending on the development of the babies and what my doctor says, I could be lying around for up to four more weeks." She made a face. "I vote for sooner, not later. It's been too long since I've seen you."

"And I apologize. Between getting ready to open the store and dealing with Grandpop, life has been a little hectic. Brought you something."

Her eyes widened. "What is it?"

"Open it and find out."

"A sudoku book." Beaming as if she'd won a prize, she paged through it. "Lots of challenger puzzles, too. How did you know I needed a new one?"

"Just a hunch. Have you talked to Grandpop recently?"

"He called this morning to check on me."

"Lucky you. I haven't heard from him in a week. I've left messages but he seems to be avoiding me."

"Because you want to know how he's doing and he's in no mood to talk about himself. He did say he's feeling better by the day, but other than that he ignored my questions. Are he and Caroline over their fight?"

"I don't think so. Vi, Caroline's granddaughter, told me she's beside herself and will probably stay in her own unit."

"Living in the same building is bound to get awkward," Whitney said. "Let's hope they mend the fences enough to be okay with that. I swear, they're as bad as high schoolers. I really miss my students. Last weekend, a group of them stopped by to visit."

"You have a knack with teens."

"I care about them, and they know it. Tell me more about Vi. Grandpop says you two keep poking your noses into his business."

"That's true. We don't want them to get married so quickly. But they're both so miserable we're rethinking that. Vi's good people. She saw you once with me when we had lunch with Grandpop one time and thought you were my wife."

"That's funny. I'd like to meet the woman whose grandma might marry our grandpa—if they make up."

"I wouldn't count on that."

"Still, I could use the company."

"She's real busy at work, but I'm sure she'd be happy to stop by." As long as she understood that Whitney had suggested it. He didn't want her getting any ideas about a long-term relationship. "I'll let her know."

"Okay. Any idea when?"

He shrugged. "I'll ask next time we talk to each other or get together. Or I'll text her." Enough talking about Vi. "I think I'll stop in and see Grandpop when I leave here. When I did that last week, he was grumpy and let me know he wanted me to leave. If he doesn't like it this time, too bad." First, he'd get hold of Vi and let her know. Maybe they could meet there and spend more time together.

"If I wasn't confined to bed, I'd go see him. Do he and Vi get along?"

"I don't think they've seen each other since the night of the accident. He seemed to like her well enough then."

"What about you, Blake? What do you think of her?"

Whitney stared hard at him as if trying to suss out his feelings. As close as he and his sister were, his love life was none of her business. "What kind of question is that?"

"Call me curious."

He was more than familiar with her tenacious stare and knew she'd hound him until he answered. "The more I know her, the better I like her. Satisfied?"

"Not yet. Do you see a lot of each other?"

Not as much as he wanted to. "We're both busy, but we get together when we can. She likes me, but I'm more interested in her than she is me." Although last night, she'd seemed open enough. He really liked being with her, wouldn't mind seeing her again tonight. "For now," he added so his sister didn't get any ideas. "I don't know that anything will come of it. Don't tell Grandpop."

"I won't. Nice that you're interested in Vi. I never for a second thought much for Daisy. I couldn't figure out what you saw in her."

"Right there with ya. If she hadn't ended things, I would've."

He heard a car pull into the driveway. "James is back. I'm taking off."

"Come see me again, okay?"

"I will. Bye-bye, niece and nephew," he told her bulging belly. "Take good care of your mama."

He left to go home, shower, and change out of his cycling clothes. That done, he called Vi.

She answered right away. "Hi. I was about to phone you."

"Yeah?" He smiled at that. "I enjoyed last night."

"Me, too," she said with a sweetness in her voice.

Good that they were on the same wavelength. "I want to see you again."

"That's why I started to call you. I'm heading to the 709 this afternoon. If you're free, we should meet there and strategize how to get our grandparents unstuck. Then at the very least, they might agree to be friends. They don't seem able to fix their problems by themselves."

Nothing about wanting to see him again in a more personal sense. It bothered him that she didn't respond to his comment. When he saw her, they'd talk about that first and then the grandparents. "You know how well strategizing worked last time, but it's worth another try. I can't reach Grandpop on the phone and haven't spoken to him since last weekend. Time for another surprise visit. Why don't we meet outside near the entrance."

CHAPTER 21

Vi didn't see Blake's car when she arrived at the 709, but with the lot nearly full—why was that?—he could already be there. The day had warmed considerably, enough that she'd left her jacket behind and changed into a springtime outfit. Wearing a sun hat and shades, she headed for their agreed meeting place outside the entrance. On a day like this, she was happy simply to be outdoors.

That and seeing Blake. Helping the grandparents, too, of course. Carmie's words about building self-confidence stuck with her. She straightened her back in a pose that radiated confidence and silently reminded herself that she was a warm person with a bright spirit. Beautiful too, even if she wasn't.

He was waiting for her this time in jeans and a teal-color, short-sleeve shirt similar to the one last night. In Aviator sunglasses, he could easily pass as a celebrity under cover, especially with his shaggy hair. Her heart lifted and she let out an admiring sigh. She couldn't help but remember the feel of his arms around her and his lips on hers.

As she drew closer to him, he flashed the genuine smile

that filled her with both joy and fear. Being warm with a bright spirit didn't mean she wasn't afraid of her feelings.

"You look like spring incarnate in that dress," he said.

So sweet. "Thanks. It's that kind of day."

"Let's walk and talk."

"For another strategy session, right? Other than a quick glance around, I haven't explored the grounds," she said as they started along the cement pathway in the back. "Any idea why the parking lot is so full?"

"My guess is, it's a mixture of the weather and people wanting to visit friends and family who live here."

That made sense. Adults and kids walking the opposite direction nodded and smiled as they crossed paths. Vi loved that. "Everyone is friendly and the landscaping is so beautiful. Even the artificial lake and fountain. And look at the flowers! I had no idea there were so many here. Another reason why Gran likes this place so much. There are the tennis courts she and Malcom mentioned. This feels like a park with outdoor activities. So, what's our goal with the grandparents?"

"We'll get to that after we talk about last night."

"I thought we already did. We both enjoyed it. What else is there to say?"

Due to his shades, she couldn't see his eyes. He wasn't smiling. "Do you want to see me again?"

"Isn't that what we're doing now?"

He made a sound of disgust. "This avoidance thing you have is getting old. Every time I mention you and me—us— you either ignore me or change the subject. What's with that?"

Caught off-guard, she frowned. "Nothing, because I don't do it."

"You just did. I asked if you want to see me again and your

answer is we're seeing each other now when you know I mean in the future. Going out together, talking and getting to know more about each other, either with friends or alone like last night. Do you want that or not?"

Talk about an ambush. She flipped her sunglasses up and eyed him. "You bring that up here, around a bunch of people? For all you know, someone who recognizes us could tell Malcom or Gran. I don't want them knowing anything about us together."

"Gossip doesn't bother me. You won't talk about us when we're alone, so why not here? I can't read your mind, Vi. Let me in."

He sounded like Carmie and Rose, darn him. "I thought I did on the patio last night."

"We fooled around some, but I want to know what you're thinking."

"I, um…" Unsure what to say, she went silent.

She wanted him to let her off the hook, but he grasped her arm and steered her to an empty bench under a flowering tree. "You can't weasel out this time. Talk to me and no tricks."

By the set of his jaw, he meant business. "All right. Yes, I want to see more of you, and yes, I want to continue where we left off last night." Which was the truth. She wasn't about to share her fear that she'd end up broken-hearted, didn't want him to know she was half in love with him. "But I don't want to rush into having sex," she added, remembering another piece of wisdom from Carmie to slow down.

"Which is why we—I—stopped last night," he said.

"And a good thing. I got a little carried away."

"An easy thing to do when were alone together."

"So how are we supposed to slow down?" she asked.

"By agreeing to do it and sticking to that."

"Even when we're crazy wild for more?"

"Even then."

"Pinky swear?"

He laughed. "My sister used to make me do that. By the way, she wants to meet you."

"What?" Vi was confused. "How does she even know about me?"

"Your name came up. She's interested in meeting the granddaughter of the woman Malcom wants to marry."

"Or used to want to marry—we're still in the dark, and from what we know, things seem pretty iffy."

"With them, we can't be sure of anything. "

"We haven't discussed that yet. Isn't that why we're here?"

"Maybe I wanted to see you, too. Let's walk." They stood up and continued along the path. "If you want to meet my sister, you'll have to come to her house. She'd like that. You're good company and she's starved for contact with people."

"That's right, she's bedridden. I guess so, but it'll have to be on a weekend. I'm going to be really busy at work."

"A corporate vice president. It bears repeating that I'm proud of you."

"I'm proud of me, too." Admitting it made her feel bold and confident. She decided to use some of that self-assurance to ask a question. "At the club last night, you told Devin we're together. Why did you say it?"

"Because he needed to back off."

She'd hoped to hear something more, that he wanted them to be a couple, even for a little while. Wrong, and she tried to hide her disappointment. "That's what I thought."

"Hold on, there." His turn to push his shades up to the top of his head. "Are you saying you want us to be together?"

"You're not interested in anything long-term. I'm not sure I am, either." Untrue, but a little fib couldn't hurt. "But yes, I'd like that, as long as we keep our heads on straight." And she held on to her heart, or at least buried her feelings.

"I can get on board with that. Do you want to go riding with me sometime? I keep thinking about your comment that you used a bike mostly for chores. The ride I have in mind would be strictly fun. Hey, we should bike to see my sister."

"How far away is she?"

"A mile or two from my place. You could drive over and we'll leave from there."

Vi liked the idea. "Let's do it. I'll rent a bike from your store."

"I'm thinking you can test-drive my favorite new model, the same kind I rode to your place during that storm. I want your take on it."

"Even if I'm out of shape?"

"It'll be a good way for me to gauge whether it'd work well for all levels of cyclist."

"I'm flattered you chose me."

"She said yes!" he said and grinned. "Now, about the grandparents. You're the idea whiz kid. What's your suggestion?"

"I'm a whiz kid," she said, gleefully blowing on her fingernails and rubbing them on her upper chest.

"You sure are. Your idea to rehire employees either as temps or permanently got you a huge promotion. Tell me what you've come up with for Grandpop and Caroline."

She shared the plan she'd hatched earlier that day. "First,

we visit Gran together. Then we escort her to Malcom's unit and refuse to leave till they talk. Or vice versa."

"If they're both home."

"If not, we'll track them down."

* * *

DOUBTFUL THE GRANDPARENT counseling thing would work, but ready to give it his best, Blake headed with Vi to sign in at the front desk. Lots of activity there with Charlotte over-seeing visitors coming and going. They waited awhile for their turn.

"You'd think they were lined up to buy tickets to a concert," Vi muttered under her breath.

"There's no rush."

"I can't help it," she said again in the low voice. "I want to get this done."

"And we will," he assured her, directly into her ear. She wore small earrings with cat faces, the same size as her pale yellow earring flowers last night. He'd noticed them when he'd kissed her just below the earlobe and she'd tilted her head for him. "Cute kitty earrings," he added, close enough that his lips brushed the sensitive place.

Vi shivered, and the urge to plant a lingering kiss there grabbed hold of him. She pulled away. "Stop," she scolded, all no-nonsense.

She had a point. He behaved himself. At last, they took their turn at the desk. He greeted Charlotte with his usual grin. "Don't you ever take a day off?" he asked as he signed in.

"I'm filling in for Dean. His daughter's getting married this afternoon. Don't you love weddings?" She smiled at them.

If she thought he and Vi were headed that direction, she was mistaken. "They're all right. You remember Vi."

"Of course. I haven't seen you since last week, Vi. Welcome back."

"Thanks. It sure is busy today."

"You know how weekends can be."

Despite the line of people waiting to sign in, there was no one at the elevator. Eager to get Vi alone for a few minutes, he nudged her into the empty car as soon as the door opened.

"Now who's in a rush?" she asked.

"I am." Usually slow elevators bugged him. Not today. Refusing to waste a second, he pulled her close for a string of sizzling kisses. By the time the car beeped their arrival at the sixth floor, he was way too turned on.

"What was that for?" she asked, looking dazed. "I thought we agreed to slow down."

"It's not like we're doing anything wild. We're seeing each other and had a little time to ourselves, so why not make good use of it? Also, we needed a distraction before we meet with our grandparents. This is the first time, and as prickly as they both are, things could get dicey."

"No, Blake, not the first time. At dinner the night they sprung their engagement on us, then again at the Sea Captain's Café."

"But we haven't gone as a couple to visit them here in their units."

"I don't know that I'd call us a couple," she said.

"What would you call it?"

"Seeing each other, period. To me, the word 'couple' signifies a commitment we don't have."

Talk about nitpicky. "In my book, if we're seeing each

other, we're in a relationship, which qualifies as a couple. You okay with that?"

"I guess," Vi said. "Call it what you want as long as they don't get any ideas about this thing between us. Their attention ought to be focused on making up and reconnecting, not on you and me. I think we should see Gran first. Malcom's more stubborn than she is and might not want to go to her unit."

"Fine with me." Vi's hair needed combing. "Hold still," he said and smoothed it for her. "Better, but you might want to check for yourself."

She dug in her purse for a comb and mirror. "What's wrong with it?"

"It looks like we've been in bed together." She blushed, which was cute. "I wish I didn't have flyaway hair. That's why I wear it pulled back at work. Yours is nice and thick. I envy that."

"Feel free to run your fingers through it any time. One more thing." The hallway was deserted, but to be safe, he backed her behind a large plant before kissing her again.

Despite her dreamy expression, she made an exasperated sound. "You're crazy, know that?"

"I like kissing you." She didn't reply. "I like kissing you," he repeated, raising his eyebrows.

"Oh, you expect me to comment. It's not easy to pull myself together after such mind-blowing kisses." She flashed a bright smile. "Is that good enough?"

"I'll take it. Ready?"

She nodded. "Good luck to both of us."

They made their way to Caroline's door. Vi rang the doorbell, waited, and then knocked twice. No answer. "Maybe she's in the bathroom."

"Or she went out."

"I'll try her cell phone." She punched in the number. After a moment, she sighed. "She's not answering. Wherever she is, I'll bet her phone's off. I wish she'd remember to turn it on. Hi, Gran. I stopped by to see you but you're out and not answering your phone. Call me, okay?" She disconnected and blew out a frustrated breath. "Well, crap."

"I hear that. Let's go to Grandpop's place."

Again, no one answered the door. This time, Blake made the call. "I'll put it on speaker," he said. To his surprise, his grandfather answered after three rings. "Hello, Blake."

He didn't sound at all happy about the call. Blake heard voices and a few unrecognizable noises in the background. "Where are you?"

"At the Mercedes dealership, looking at new models. They're searching for another gold one. If they don't find it, they'll repaint the one I buy. Hold on." Grandpop muted his phone, then came back. "I have to go."

"When will you be home?" Blake asked, but the man had disconnected. He shook his head. "The night of the accident he said he wanted to buy a new car, but I didn't expect him to go out looking this soon. It hasn't been that long since the accident."

"If he's shopping today, he must be feeling a lot better. We know where Malcom is. Now we have to find Gran."

"Let's drive to the Mercedes showroom and find out if he knows anything."

They entered the elevator and punched the ground floor. Alone this time, too, Blake reached for Vi. But the elevator pinged and stopped on the fifth floor, putting an end to another steamy kiss. As the door slid open, they jerked apart.

He recognized the man and woman who entered. They seemed both surprised and extremely interested, and he figured they'd caught a glimpse of him and Vi in action. Talk about embarrassing.

"Hi," he said. "I'm Malcom's grandson, Blake. Meet Vi."

"Caroline's daughter," she clarified.

"Hello, Vi. We're Bud and Connie Henderson."

"Are you two in a relationship?" Connie asked.

Blake preferred not to answer. "Nice out today," he said. "We'd hoped to stop in and say hello, but both our grandparents are out. I was able to reach Malcom."

"But I can't reach Caroline," Vi said. "She's not home and not answering her phone."

"I haven't seen either of them." Connie smiled as if she knew a secret. "I'm sure they'll turn up somewhere."

"What's up with people shooting us mysterious smiles?" Blake asked. "Do they know something we don't?"

"It's like they think we're in a serious relationship, We're not."

"You're right about that."

CHAPTER 22

"I'll drive," Blake offered as he and Vi signed out and left the 709.

Vi was fine with that. "I've never kissed anyone in an elevator," she admitted on the way to the Mercedes dealership.

He grinned at her. "Sure was fun."

"I thought so." But sticking to kisses, period, was frustratingly unsatisfying, like starving for days, then sampling a mouth-watering appetizer with no other food in sight. If she weren't careful, she'd throw caution to the winds and have sex soon, when she wasn't ready.

Or was she?

Ready or not, the way she ached for him meant holding off much longer was doubtful. Now that she and Blake were in a relationship of sorts, it made sense. As long as she remembered not to expect any promises of a future together, which she didn't, she ought to be okay. This was not the time to decide, and she shoved her thoughts and longing aside until later.

Traffic was light, and they soon passed the first of three different dealerships. "The population here is about twenty-five thousand," she said. "I've always wondered how these dealerships survive."

Blake shrugged. "No idea, but they do. There it is, up ahead." He nodded at the tall blue sign with the three-pointed star and pulled into the lot. "Let's go find Grandpop."

Locating him wasn't difficult. He was seated at a table, engaged in an intent conversation with a salesperson. The man left and headed for someone's office. "Hey, Grandpop," Blake said.

Malcom's frown included both him and Vi. "What are you two doing here?"

"Yes, it's good to see you, too," Blake said as if the man had greeted them with a pleased smile. "If you're out and about, you must be feeling pretty good."

"Still sore, but much better." He nodded at Vi. "Hello."

"Hi, Malcom. I'm trying to find Gran."

"We don't know where she is, and you hung up on me before I could ask. At least you answered the phone. What's the deal?"

"I've been busy." Suddenly, Malcom's face lit up. "Here she comes."

Vi followed his gaze, saw Gran and was shocked. "You two made up?"

"We did."

Blake looked stunned. "Why didn't you tell us?"

"You didn't ask."

"How could we, when you refused to answer your phones?"

"Well, hello." Gran nodded at them. "What are you two doing here?"

"Malcom asked us the same thing," Vi said. "The better question is why are *you*, Gran?"

"I'm keeping Malcom company while he negotiates a better price for his new Mercedes. He's really good at that."

Malcom beamed. "Almost as good as you."

Whatever that meant. "The last time you and I spoke, Gran, you and Malcom were still mad at each other," Vi reminded her. "What changed?"

Her grandmother squinted at her as if she'd asked a ridiculous question. "We talked it out and made up, like any couple does. The day my insurance check arrived, I signed it over to him."

He nodded. "We went to the bank and deposited it."

Without a word to Vi or Blake. "All this time, I worried about that check, Gran. When did it come, and why didn't you tell me?"

"On Tuesday. How was I supposed to know you expected a call. Why would I? It's my business, not yours. As soon as Malcom deposited the money, we went straight to the finance department at the 709 and signed the documents for our new unit."

"Back up," Blake said. "What brought you around, Grandpop?"

The man gave Blake a *you-have-to-ask?* look. "I love her, I missed her and I can't live without her. I've always appreciated a challenge, and she drives a hard bargain." He winked at Blake and Vi. "She's tougher than I am."

"That's why you love me," Gran said, beaming.

"One of many reasons."

They shared a brief kiss. Vi hoped they behaved better than they had at the Sea Captain's Table. To her relief, they settled down.

Clearly, they didn't appreciate her and Blake being there. She wanted to leave and process their abrupt about-face. "They're conducting business, Blake. We should go."

"Not until they clarify a few things."

"Such as?" Malcom asked.

"I don't buy the excuse that we didn't ask so you didn't tell. What's your real reason for keeping us in the dark?"

Malcom gestured at Gran to answer. "You two are so dead-set against us getting married, that frankly, we didn't care to deal with your attitudes."

"That's not true," Vi said. "Well maybe at first, because you'd just met and were moving so quickly when you barely knew each other. But we came around. Of course, you didn't know because you couldn't be bothered answering your phones."

Gran opened her mouth to say who knew what, but Blake spoke first. "When are you two getting married?"

The seniors clasped hands and smiled at each other like besotted lovers. "A week from today," Caroline said, then lowered her voice. "The 709 has agreed to let us move in together a few days before the wedding, as they need to get our current units in shape for new residents. We have a lot to do to get ready."

"Are we the only ones who didn't know?" Vi asked. With Malcom suddenly fascinated by the nondescript floor and Gran wearing a guilty expression, she had the answer. "We were." That explained the cryptic smiles at the 709 earlier. "Are we invited to the wedding?"

Blake narrowed his eyes. "You damn well better say yes."

The salesperson headed toward them. "We'll talk about this later," Malcom said, dismissing them with a flick of his hand.

"Fine. Let's get out of here, Vi. Apologies for Grandpop's behavior," he said on the way out. "At times, he's rough around the edges. But you know that from the call I made from the new store about meeting them for dinner."

"As you heard, Gran isn't always agreeable, either. That doesn't bother me, but the way they cut us out but told other people hurts my feelings. We don't even know if they plan to invite us to the wedding."

* * *

THE FEW DAYS following the surprising news from Malcom and Caroline were busy for Blake. Now that spring had hit, business was through the roof at the original BW Bikes. If that wasn't enough, there was still plenty to do before the second store opened. Vi was constantly on his mind. She was equally busy, learning the ins and outs of her new job. Despite the long hours that stretched from early morning till late at night for both of them, they managed to keep in touch by phone and text.

In the middle of the week, she called him before noon, a first. Had something happened? "Everything okay?" he asked.

"Not really. I'm dealing with nonstop questions and problems I'm not sure how to handle. My secretary Linda is a big help, but she has her own work to do. I'm sure I'm driving both her and Todd nuts with questions of my own. For the sake of my sanity, I need to get out of here. I'm leaving early today, and I'd love to see you. Can we get together, or are you too busy?"

Music to his ears. "Forget busy. This is a day made for a bike ride. Let's do it. I was just thinking about you."

"Oh?" She sounded pleased.

"I'm at the original bike store right now. You can meet Joanie, who'll be my second-in-command at the new store once it opens, and Ross, here to help with the nonstop flow of customers. He knows the ropes. They'll be fine without me. The sun sets tonight around eight, and I doubt you'll want to ride in the dark. Meet me here a couple hours before then, or earlier if you can. We'll ride and have dinner after."

"That sounds perfect."

"If you need cycling clothes, we have a great selection here."

"I found that out on Sunday, when I came in and picked up a few things."

"I wish you'd called and let me know. I'd have met you here."

"I needed to do some thinking by myself."

About what? She'd tell him if and when she wanted to, he figured. She arrived shortly after two in heels and a killer spring dress that showed off her sexy legs. He loved looking at them, loved looking at her, period. After a second or two, he pulled his gaze to hers and cleared his throat. "You're earlier than I expected."

"Too early?" she asked, touching the back of her head, where she'd fixed her hair in a fancy twist at the nape.

"Let me introduce you to Joanie and Ross. Meet Vi."

Joanie, who was roughly ten years older than Vi, and Ross, about their age, smiled at her. "Good to meet you," Joanie said.

"You, too. Blake has mentioned you. You'll be his second-in-command at the new store." She turned to Ross. "He's talked about you, too. You're the new HR person, and you guys ride together."

"That's me," Ross said. "I've heard good things about you."

She blushed a little, then showed Blake her gym bag. "Where should I change?"

"Use one of the empty fitting rooms."

In the bathroom, he donned his standard biking attire, then waited for her. Moments later, she emerged from the fitting room in a red and black cycling jersey and black padded shorts.

Slender with soft curves, she had a body made for the snug clothing. The outfit turned him on, but then, most things about her did. By Ross's appreciative look, he also liked what he saw. Good thing he was involved with someone or Blake might've felt threatened.

"I finally heard from Gran about the wedding," she said as they wheeled the bikes outside. "We're invited. So are Rose and Peter. Gran said she'd call you next."

"She did, but I was away from my phone. She left a message."

"Did she give you the details? The wedding starts at two on Saturday and will be in the back garden—I don't think we saw that when we took a walk around last weekend, although I may have seen it from Gran's window. Anyway, during the ceremony, that section of the grounds will be closed."

"Too bad Whitney can't make it," he said. "I promised to take photos and a video or two."

Standing in the sun outside, they donned helmets. By now,

he recognized when Vi was on-edge. "Nervous about the ride?" he asked.

"A little, but more excited. I'm so looking forward to forgetting about work for a while."

"That bad, huh?"

"Nonstop phone calls and—never mind. I don't even want to think about it, okay?"

"You won't, guaranteed." He gave her the Bad Boy and used an older bike he liked, and they set out.

They stuck to an easy bike trail. He didn't travel too fast, and she had no trouble keeping up. "There's a rest stop just ahead," he said some twenty minutes later.

"Thank goodness. I need a break."

While they rested, she drank what was left in her water bottle and refilled it from the fountain provided for anyone in need of it, then used the facilities. "I'm ready to go now."

"Having a good time?"

"This is wonderful. I wish I were in better shape so you didn't have to go slowly."

Nothing wrong with her shape. "I don't mind at all. Ride regularly, and you'll get there."

"Define regularly."

"Once or twice a week if possible."

"If I can squeeze in the time, I will."

"No reason you can't ride Saturdays or Sundays or after work. I'll go with you. Let's stop for today and head back."

At the store, they parked the bikes and went inside to collect their clothes.

She wrinkled her nose. "I don't want to change until I shower."

"Same here. I have two full bathrooms at my place, remember? We'll clean up there, then go have dinner."

CHAPTER 23

V i was supposed to be taking a shower in Blake's bathroom on the main floor. Instead, she stood in the hallway and thought about what she'd decided about her and Blake, what she wanted more than anything. She was ready to have sex. All she needed now was to go upstairs, take off her clothes, and join him in the shower. The idea turned her on but also scared her. Better not. She took off her shoes. Suddenly her phone rang. Linda. Her secretary knew she was taking the afternoon off. Ignoring it, Vi toed out of her sneakers. The darn thing rang again. "Shoot," she muttered and answered. "Yes, Linda?"

"Sorry to bother you, but I have a question only you can answer."

By the time the conversation ended, the shower upstairs had gone quiet. Too late to surprise Blake. Best to talk to him about it first? Vi wasn't sure, and anyway the opportunity to surprise him had passed. She shut the door to the bathroom and stepped alone into the shower.

It wasn't until she was out again, drying herself off that she realized the gym bag with her work clothes was where she'd dropped it in the living room. Wrapping the towel around herself, she exited the bathroom to get it. Blake happened to be coming down the stairs, dressed and barefoot, his hair wet and combed back.

"What do we have here?" His avid gaze flickered over her, and she wanted him even more.

Yet she wasn't quite ready to divulge the plan that hadn't happened. "I left my gym bag in the living room and was about to get it."

"I'll do that."

In the seconds he was gone, she realized she hadn't missed the opportunity she wanted after all. It'd simply changed from the shower to some other place. Hmm...

He returned, bag in hand. "Here you go."

"I don't need my clothes just yet." She let the towel slip down a little.

His eyes were dark pools of lust. "What're you doing, Vi?"

"Exactly what it looks like. Seducing you."

He let his gaze comb over her. Hair loose and sexy, towel hovering mere inches below her crotch, the legs he so liked slightly apart, tops of her breasts peeking from the upper edge of the towel... No man in his right mind could resist that. He swallowed and hardly aware of his actions, started toward her. She was trembling. Primed and ready as he was to love her, he stopped short of her and scrubbed his hand over his face.

Her expression changed from sexy and aroused to mortified. "I thought... if you don't want me..."

"Oh, I want you." He glanced down at the bulge in his jeans. "I think about making love to you day and night, but this is so sudden. Last time we talked, you said kisses only. Yeah, we went a little farther on the deck. Now, you say you're ready for the full deal. Sure about that?"

"Are you trying to talk me out of having sex with you? I've been thinking about it since we left the Mercedes dealership. I want this, Blake."

"But you're shaking."

"Because I need you. And yes, I'm just out of the shower and cold. Warm me up?"

"Not until we talk." He stepped into the bathroom, took a clean towel from one of the drawers, and draped it over her shoulders. "I don't have condoms on me, but there are some upstairs."

"That's okay. I'm on the pill. And I'm clean."

"Me, too. Yes, we're seeing each other, but I don't want you getting the wrong idea. What I mean is, I don't want to hurt you."

She scoffed. "If you think I'm falling in love with you, think again. I'm glad we're together for now, but I understand there are no promises of anything serious. I haven't had sex in almost a year and I happen to want it with you." Her chin jutted up, all proud and beautiful. She took his breath away. "Does that meet with your approval?"

He answered with a sizzling kiss.

* * *

BLAKE'S KISS blazed through every inch of Vi's body. She let the towels fall away. He stared at her, trailed his hands down her breasts to her nipples. "You're beautiful."

With his expression almost reverent, she half believed him.

219

But that was the passion talking. "I don't want to be the only naked person here," she said and lifted the hem of his shirt. He stopped her and shed it himself. She'd seen him bare-chested the night of the ferocious rain storm. "You're the beautiful one here, at least the part I can see."

"Easy fix for that." He unzipped his fly and stepped out of his jeans and boxers. He was gloriously aroused.

"Oh, my," she said.

He started to kiss her again. "Wait," she said. "Are we going to have sex here in the hallway?"

He let out a low laugh and grabbed her hand. "My bedroom. Now."

On the way upstairs, they stopped frequently to kiss. By the time he tugged her into his room, she was more than ready. Dusk had fallen, and she noted the bed was made. He let go of her to jerk the comforter back before they tumbled onto the sheets. "Right where I want you at last," he said.

He kissed her mouth, then worked his way to her throat, her upper chest and finally her breasts. "I have to taste those perfect breasts now."

He took a nipple into his mouth. Pleasure swept her away, and all that mattered was him. He slowly explored his way down her body. Restless, she urged him lower. At last, he focused on the part of her that ached for release. His lips, tongue and fingers drove her wild, and she arched up. "I'm about to climax."

"Go for it," he said, and did something with his mouth and fingers that pushed her over the brink.

She called out and lost herself in powerful sensations she hadn't known were possible. When it was over, she lay spent.

"I think you liked that," he said, smiling and smoothing her hair back.

"Understatement of the world. I loved it." She let her hand drift over his broad chest and flat belly, then down further. He sucked in a breath and went still. "I think you like this, too," she said, stroking him. Wanting to give him the same enjoyable release she'd had, she put her head down close.

In a flash, she was on her back. "No fair," she said. "This is supposed to be your turn."

"Save it for later. Right now, I need to be inside you."

She wanted that, too. "Then don't keep me waiting."

Within moments a second orgasm hit. This one even better because they climaxed together.

After, they lay entwined the way lovers did in the movies. "We're a good match," Blake said.

"Really good. You totally took my mind off work."

"I'd hope so." He planted a tender kiss on her mouth. "I'll be right back." Dusk had become night and the room was dark. The hallway light was on, though, and she watched him pad out of the room toward the bathroom without a hint of modesty. A glorious male, sure of himself.

She liked him a lot. Or so she told herself, but a feeling dangerously close to love flooded her heart. Close? She was already there. Something she'd never admit to him, couldn't. He didn't feel the same way, and saying it out loud was too risky. Not about to lie in his bed waiting for him to come back like the lovesick fool she was, she sat up.

He was a stupendous lover, and for now that was enough. His interest in her wouldn't last forever. When it ended, her heart would surely break. Regardless, she intended to enjoy being with him for as long as it lasted.

CHAPTER 24

Having cleaned up in the bathroom, Blake returned to the bedroom with a warm washcloth and towel for Vi. She wasn't there. Huh. "Vi?" he called out. "Where'd you go?"

"I'm in the living room."

Wondering at that, he descended the stairs. "I brought you a washcloth and towel," he said, holding them out.

"That's so sweet. I took care of myself in the bathroom down here."

She seemed okay, but he sensed she'd pulled away, although he couldn't put his finger on what was different. She was dressed in the outfit she'd worn to the store that afternoon, which made sense. It was that or dirty cycling clothes.

Disappointment flooded him. He wanted to have sex again. Apparently, she'd had enough. Must be having regrets.

"You're sorry about the sex. Maybe we should've waited longer before we jumped into bed."

"Are you deaf? I said it was great, and I meant that. Really, the best I've ever had."

Her smile and the words eased his misgivings, yet she still

seemed somewhat distant. "I agree, it was way up there. I love your body and the way you respond to me. You're a dynamo in bed."

"I am?"

"The way you took charge and let me know what you wanted, then when you climaxed? Super-hot. No one has mentioned that to you?"

"No, but the guys I've been with never turned me on much."

Weird. "Because?"

"They were more interested in themselves than me. But you're not like that."

"If you want to do this again, I'm available now."

"I can't, Blake. I have to get up early tomorrow and should probably get home."

That made sense, even if it wasn't what he wanted to hear. "Not without eating something first. It's way past dinnertime, and I'm sure your belly's as empty as mine."

"Yes, I'm starving, but sitting in a restaurant or waiting for takeout could take a while."

"Forget that. Why don't we grab something to eat on the way to your car. Burgers, hotdogs, tacos or whatever, if that works for you."

She licked her lips. "Let's do that." On the drive, they chatted. "I feel so much better than I did when I left work. The bike ride, making love..."

"I enjoyed all of it, too. We should do this again soon."

"I agree."

They pulled into a fast food place, ordered from the car and ate in the Lexus, wolfing their meals in record time. "A cheeseburger and onion rings—exactly what I needed," she said as she crumpled the paper and put it in the bag that'd contained their orders. "Sorry to eat and run."

"I get it. I should go to bed early myself."

He pulled up to her car. "When will I see you again?"

"Not until Saturday. I'll probably work that morning just to keep up, but I'll be done well ahead of the wedding."

"Let's carpool. I'll pick you up." If all went well, after the festivities they'd spend a few dynamite hours together.

"Okay. See you then."

She leaned in and kissed him lightly before exiting the car, a brief brush of the lips that left him hungry for more. Moments later, she was gone.

On the drive home, he thought again about the subtle changes in her he didn't understand. Most of the women he'd been with tended to hold on tight, often signaling they wanted to stay the night or out-and-out asking. Since Sammi, he rarely spent a full night with anyone. He didn't want a clingy woman, which Vi wasn't.

He didn't doubt for a second that she liked him. His confusion stemmed from the changes after she'd dressed, when the warmth and affection she'd shown him for weeks had cooled. More mixed messages.

What was up with that? He wanted to know. Sooner or later, he'd find out.

* * *

To Vi's amazement, the first week in her new position ended on a high note. Yes, she was tired, but the job was going better than she'd expected. Mr. Iglesias was pleased with her, Todd called her a natural leader, and Linda said she was great to work for. Positive feedback that boosted her confidence. Extra bonus: she didn't need to go to the office Saturday morning after all, which meant catching up on rest and sleeping in.

Now, if she could just stop thinking about Blake... She needed to talk to someone. Not Rose—she didn't need more advice from her little sister. Carmie didn't answer her phone. No doubt she was doing something with Chris. Vi left a message. After dinner, she fell asleep and slept until morning.

As she finished dressing for the wedding, her friend phoned her back. "Hey, you. Got your message. Chris and I were out last night. We went back to the Highway Club for comedy night, which has been switched to Fridays, and had a great time. What's going on with you? How was your first week at the new job?"

"Surprisingly good. Mr. Iglesias is happy with the way I'm quickly adjusting."

"I expected no less."

"Thanks. Gran and Malcom are getting married in a little while. Blake and I are carpooling." Vi glanced at her watch. "He's picking me up soon."

"Are you worried about the wedding?"

"It'll be interesting, but we're resigned to whatever happens."

"How are things with him?"

"That's why I called. A few nights ago, I slept with him."

"You said you might. And?"

"It was amazing, but—" Vi broke off.

"But what?"

"I'm not falling for him anymore. I'm totally in love with him, and that's a problem."

"Does he know?"

"No, and he never will."

"Ah, you're still afraid he'll leave you."

"That's a given, but I want to have sex with him again. I'm already looking forward to being with him after the wedding. Am I crazy for enjoying it while it lasts?"

"I think you know the answer to that."

"Yes, but I want your opinion anyway."

"All right. No, I don't think you're crazy. If it were me, I'd do exactly what you're doing. If you keep a level head about the future, you might not even get hurt."

Too late for that. The doorbell chimed and Vi's heart lifted. "He's here."

CHAPTER 25

After several days away from Vi, Blake was hungry to be together. "Hi," he said, feasting his eyes on her.

Today her hair was loose and parted with a red flower clip securing one side. The same color as the tiny red flowers along the hem and short sleeves of her light blue dress. Her shoes were open at the toe, revealing scarlet toenails. He really liked that.

He pulled her into a hug and kissed her. When he let her go, she wore the dreamy look he so liked. "You look beautiful."

She smiled. "Thanks. You're not so bad yourself."

In honor of the day, he'd worn a pressed shirt and dark pants. Mr. T sashayed over. "You're expecting a treat, huh. Here you go." He dropped a catnip ball at the tom's feet.

"You spoil him rotten," Vi said. "We should go. I filled his dish with cat food. Be a good boy, okay?"

The usual warmth and friendliness radiated from her, and it dawned on Blake that fatigue had been to blame for whatever had bothered her the other night. "You got some rest," he said.

"I did. As it turned out, I didn't have to work this morning and was able to sleep in. Do I look rested?"

"That and you seem more energetic. How's the job going?"

"Pretty well. Not nearly as hectic as the last time I saw you."

"That's good news." They buckled in and he headed out.

"Gran hasn't said much about the wedding except that lots of their friends from the 709 are coming," she told him on the drive. "I have no idea what to expect."

"With our grandparents, you never know. Let's hope they don't get into a fight."

Vi's eyes widened. "They wouldn't dare."

"How long is this thing supposed to last?"

"Long enough to serve a buffet dinner. Why?"

"I told Whitney we'd stop by later this afternoon."

"You mentioned that before, but I didn't know you meant today." Vi frowned. "I didn't bring my bike clothes."

"We're not riding today—we'll do that another time. My sister's super impatient for us to get to her house and share the wedding details ASAP. I promised we'd come over as soon as we leave the 709. She's looking forward to meeting you."

Vi eyed him. "What've you told her besides my name?"

"That I like you." He winked. "Are you interested in spending the evening together after we get our obligations out of the way?" he said, eager to be alone with her.

"I'm planning on it. This time at my house."

He smiled. The day was getting better by the minute.

As soon as they parked at the 709, they headed toward the gardens. "Look," Vi said and pointed ahead. "There are Rose and Peter."

Blake studied the tall, silver-haired male at her side. "So that's her husband. He looks quite a bit older than she is."

"By fifteen years." Vi spoke softly. "This is his third marriage." In a louder voice, she called out to Rose.

Her sister turned toward her and waited for them to catch up. "Hello, you two. You look a lot different from the last time I saw you, Blake. Meet my husband, Peter."

"You're the guy wearing Vi's happy coat," Peter said.

"Rose told you?" Blake didn't hide his pained expression, and the man chuckled.

Their small group headed along the path. "I wonder where the back garden is," Vi said.

Blake pointed it out. "See the tall laurel hedge on your left? It's behind there. The space is used for parties and celebrations." He tucked a lock of her hair behind the ear without the flower, trailing his finger to the sensitive place below her earlobe. He welcomed her shiver and looked forward to making her wild again. But that would have to wait.

A uniformed man and woman stood guard at the entrance to the hedge. As soon as they checked the names off the guest list, the four of them were allowed entrance.

Vi glanced around the landscaped yard and gardens. "This is every bit as pretty as the regular grounds."

A fair number of people had already gathered. All seniors from the 709, Blake guessed. No sign of Grandpop or Caroline.

"I don't even know who's marrying them," Vi told them. "The only thing she said was not to dress up. I wonder where we're supposed to sit?"

"As family members, I'd imagine up front," Peter said.

He was right. Seats bearing their names had been reserved

for them. Shortly after they sat down, two elderly women approached and introduced themselves as Karen and Suzanne.

"Friends of Caroline," one of them said.

"Gran mentioned you two," Vi commented. "It's good to meet you."

Holding a cordless microphone, a balding male named Karl, who Blake had met before, stepped in the front of the rows of chairs. "Welcome, all. The nuptials are about to begin. Our own Babette Smith has been certified online and will officiate today." The gray-haired females standing next to Karl nodded and smiled. "After the ceremony, please join us for a buffet supper at the tables to your right." As soon as Karl took his seat, a quartet consisting of retired musicians from the 709 struck up a classical piece.

Dressed in a suit and tie, a beaming Grandpop was first up the aisle. He took his place near Babette. Equally radiant and wearing a flowery dress, Caroline followed.

The ceremony was short and joyous. Without a thought, Blake reached for Vi's hand. They smiled at each other. She no longer seemed worried that people would talk about them, or if she was she didn't show it. Tears filled her eyes and the expression on her face was somber.

"You're sad," he said. "This is a happy occasion."

"Just a little sentimental." She wiped her eyes.

Rose gave her a fond smile. "She's always been softhearted, even cries at weddings on TV shows and movies."

A side of her he hadn't known about.

A reception followed. Vi and Rose congratulated Caroline and Grandpop, then hugged them both. Blake did the same. Caroline's knowing look clued him in that she'd noticed Vi and him holding hands. "What'd I tell you, Malcom? They're together. I knew you two would be. You fell in love fast, like we did."

"We're not in love," Blake and Vi stated at the same time.

Other guests crowded in, wanting to chat with the newlyweds. Not long after, the buffet opened and guests ate. When Caroline and Malcom rose and signaled they were finished, almost everyone stood.

Blake's cue to leave with Vi. Eager to get going—the sooner they left and visited Whitney and James, the sooner they could be alone—he said goodbye to the grandparents and other people. "Whitney asked me to come over and tell her all about the wedding, as soon as possible," he told them.

"Let her know we missed her and give her a kiss from us," Caroline said. "Don't be strangers, now. Malcom and I are spending two weeks in Palm Desert, but promise you'll have dinner with us when we get back."

With the second store opening in a mere four days, Blake was disappointed to hear that. "You're not coming to the grand opening of the new store?"

"When we made our reservations, we weren't thinking about that," Grandpop said. "You know how proud I am of you. We'll come see the store later."

Vi hugged Rose, Blake shook hands with Peter, and they left.

"That was nice," she said on the way to the car.

"I especially liked how short it was."

"Blake!" She elbowed him. "Keep your voice down."

"Just sayin' what everyone else was thinking."

"From what I saw, people enjoyed themselves."

"The food helped."

She rolled her eyes, then laughed. "You're incorrigible."

"One of the many reasons why you like me. Let's go see Whitney."

Then they could be alone.

* * *

THE RIDE to Whitney's house was stress-free, exactly what Vi needed. She and Blake talked about the wedding and the various people who'd come. He teased her about being sad and sentimental. Which she was, but there was more to the story. As emotional and beautiful as it was to witness the love between Gran and Malcom and listen to their deeply-felt vows, the whole thing had made her heart ache. She wanted that kind of love, wanted to make vows with a man who adored her and was committed to a lifetime together.

Unfortunately, Blake was the only man she was interested in. He'd made it more than clear that he wasn't ready for that kind of commitment and might never be.

She wasn't about to waste time wishing he'd fall in love with her someday. So no, unless she met someone as right for her as Blake there was no chance of a wedding for her. Imagining herself alone for the rest of her life made her sad all over again.

He glanced at her. "Twenty bucks for your thoughts."

"Twenty?"

"For inflation." He grinned.

"Are you upset that Gran and Malcom won't be at your grand opening?"

"Not really. Grandpop has done so much for me. I know he's pleased with my success."

"I was also thinking about Gran and Malcom and how happy they seem." Afraid she might break into tears again, she lightened up. This wasn't the time for a self-pity party. "It's nice they're taking a honeymoon—as long as I don't think about what they'll be doing during it." She made a face.

As she'd expected, Blake laughed. "We're almost at Whitney and James's place. I don't know about you, but I'm peopled out. Let's not stay long."

"But she's your sister, Blake."

"And I see her often. Don't worry, you'll have time to chat." He gave her a wicked grin. "I'm more interested in getting you all to myself."

CHAPTER 26

"I like Whitney and James," Vi commented when Blake ushered her out the couple's door sometime later. "They seem devoted to each other."

As Blake had figured, she and his sister had bonded fast. "They're good people."

"I enjoyed telling them about the wedding. And those photos. Wow, Blake. Is there anything you're not good at?"

He chuckled. "Careful, or I'll get a swelled head. Credit my smart phone for the pictures. Taking them gave me something to do at the wedding."

Her look was pure *you can't fool me*. "You liked the ceremony, and you know it."

She knew him so well.

"They loved every photo. You should make a special album for them and for Gran and Malcom."

"That's a great idea. It'll have to wait till after the grand opening."

"Whitney's belly is enormous, and she's not quite thirty-two weeks along. It's obvious she's sick and tired of bed rest.

She's looking forward to visiting her doctor next week. She really wants—"

Blake tuned out the rest of her chatter. His mind was on other things. Namely, getting to Vi's house and into bed.

"You stopped listening," she said with the little creases between her brows. "Where did you go?"

The road was empty of traffic, and he signaled, then pulled to the side of the road.

"Is there something wrong with the car?" she asked.

In answer, he leaned across the console and kissed her with feeling.

When he let go of her, her eyes were closed. She opened them and let out a soft sigh. "What was that for?"

"An appetizer for when we get to your house."

"It certainly whetted my appetite. Can't you drive a little faster?"

"I could get a ticket."

"I don't see a lot of traffic or any police officers around. Besides, which is worse, a ticket or me going up in flames with no one to douse the fire?"

He sped ahead. The instant she unlocked the front door, he tugged her inside, shoved the door closed, and got down to business. Too eager to head for the bedroom, he backed her toward the living room. "Wait," she said, breathless and sounding every bit as turned on. She stepped back to get rid of her shoes and panties.

How he wanted her. Groaning, he pulled her up close.

She toyed with his earlobe, tugging gently with her teeth. "Get rid of your pants and shorts."

Blake shed both in record time, then hiked up her dress. Cupping her soft rear end, he lifted her up.

Moaning, she wrapped her bare legs around him. He couldn't make it to the sofa, and they ended up on the carpet. He paused to pull his shirt off, wad it up, and placed it under her head. Then he entered her. She was slick with desire. No foreplay necessary. Within moments, they both climaxed.

"On a scale of one to ten, that was fifty," he said sometime later, still inside her. He'd never imagined she'd be so passionate. "I didn't plan for things to happen so fast, but it was impossible to slow down."

"I didn't mind. I wanted this every bit as badly as you."

"When you say stuff like that I get hot and bothered all over again, he said and nuzzled her neck.

Meowing plaintively, the cat sashayed toward them. They sat up, and Blake shook his head. "You have great timing, buddy." He headed into the bathroom and brought back a washcloth and hand towel.

The flush from their joining still stained her skin. Beautiful, seductive woman. Thanks to the wild sex, her hair was a mess. The flower had gone AWOL. He tweaked a lock. "What happened to the flower in your hair?"

"I'm sure it's here somewhere."

Mr. T meowed again. "He's hungry," Vi said. She stood and straightened her skirt, then picked up the tom and carried him to the kitchen.

No panties under that dress. Already, he wanted her again. As soon as he recovered. Lusting like the dog he was, he padded into the kitchen after her.

After she fed the cat, he led her upstairs to the bedroom, where they made love again at a more leisurely pace. The steamy shower sex that followed drained him. Yet at the same time, he didn't think he'd ever get enough of her.

It was going to be a long, scorching evening.

* * *

AS WONDERFUL AS sex with Blake was, after making love three times in fairly quick succession, Vi needed time to catch her breath and gather her thoughts. When he hinted at wanting another round once he recovered from the shower that had topped any fantasy, she called a halt and cinched the sash on her robe. "Let's take a break, okay? It's been a while since we last ate, and I need food."

They decided on fried egg sandwiches for dinner. "I need to wash my hands first," she told him, and padded into the bathroom. Finally, a chance to think. Standing in front of the mirror, she fixed her hair. Her skin was rosy and she looked thoroughly sated. She definitely was, had never been with anyone like him. He was passionate and generous, and seemed to enjoy exploring every inch of her body in exciting ways that kept her wanting more. Praising her for her passion and enthusiasm made her feel sexy, but also uneasy.

Was he mostly interested in her for the sex? The dismal thought put a damper on her high spirits.

Every time they came together, her love for him had grown until her heart was so full, holding back her feelings was almost painful. Which was crazy. She'd known him for a month, not long enough for such deep emotions. Yet, despite knowing the risks, she'd thrown caution to the wind and given her heart to him. If he found out... A chill shook her. He wouldn't. She couldn't bear his rejection.

The best way to protect herself was to end the relationship

before he did. As if doing that could block the heartache. At least she'd save face.

Her mind made up, she headed back into the kitchen, where Blake had already made the sandwiches. Couldn't get rid of him yet. No longer hungry, she forced the food down.

"Suddenly, you're awful quiet," he said as they finished. "You okay?"

The perfect opening to break up. But her courage flagged. "I'm fine, thanks," she lied. "Just tired. I need to get some sleep."

A small part of her half hoped he'd try to convince her to let him stay the night, which proved what a screwed-up mess she was.

He didn't even try. "I get that. This has been quite a day and an exceptional evening. There's a lot left to do yet before the grand opening. I probably won't see you until then."

She nodded. A quick kiss and he was gone.

CHAPTER 27

O ut of habit, Vi did the laundry and cleaning on Sundays, activities that left her free to think. She dreaded telling Blake they couldn't see each other anymore, but it had to be. The question was, when and where?

She could use some advice from Carmie, but as she unloaded the groceries she'd bought that afternoon, Rose phoned. "What was your opinion of that wedding?" she asked.

"I thought it was sweet." Although Rose couldn't see her, she smiled. "You?"

"It was wonderful. Gran looked radiant, and Malcom seems totally gone on her."

"The food was tasty, too," Vi said. "It was good to see Peter."

"I was happy about that and hoped we could spend today together, but he's gone to the hospital. On a Sunday." Rose blew out a loud breath. "That man…"

"He's dedicated to his work."

"Yes, and I should be used to that by now. I noticed you and Blake holding hands during the ceremony."

"So that's why you called."

"Don't sound surprised. You're my big sister, and I want details. Are you two a thing now?"

Vi didn't want to discuss that with Rose just yet. To her relief, her phone beeped, signaling a call from Carmie. "That's Carmie. Bye." She clicked over to her bestie. "I'm glad you called. How did you know I wanted to touch base?"

"Tell me about the wedding."

"I really enjoyed it." Vi shared the details.

"You've just convinced me to have an outdoor wedding," Carmie said.

"Will Chris go for that?"

"He'd elope if I agreed to it, but I know he'll like the idea. What did Blake think of the wedding, and how are things with him?"

Vi told her about meeting Whitney and then ending up at the townhouse. "We had sex again."

"Once you start, it's hard to stop."

"It certainly was last night."

"Ah, you had it more than once."

"Three times."

"Nice," Carmie said. "Did he sleep over?

"I thought about it but didn't give him a chance to ask."

"Why not?"

"I was worn out. Also, I'm in love with him."

"When we met for coffee, you said you might be. What's wrong with that? From what you say, he seems very inter-ested in you."

"About having sex with me, definitely. Love? Nope."

"The two go hand-in-hand, you know."

"Not always. It's obvious he likes me, but I'd bet my job his feelings for me aren't half as strong as mine for him. I don't expect him to change."

"Why would you say that? You can't predict the future."

"No, but a while ago, he told me he doubted he could commit to anyone for long."

"That was then, this is now. You haven't known each other long. You fell for him fast. Maybe he needs time to figure it out. Better yet, why not talk to him and tell him how you feel?"

Vi snorted. "Are you nuts? One whiff of the L word and he'd be gone so fast… I refuse to subject myself to that. I've decided to cut things off with him."

"OMG, Vi. I wish you'd let go of the past. You're not twenty and naïve and he's not Devin."

Duh. "Excuse me for not wanting to embarrass myself."

"I hear you, but it's clear to me that this is a self-confidence issue."

"You lost me, Carmie. I don't see how any of this has to do with confidence."

"Well, it does. Have you been looking in the mirror and telling yourself you're beautiful?"

"Not really." Vi sighed. "He makes me feel that way, but it's bound to fade."

"Quit courting trouble. If you felt confident about yourself in other ways besides work, you'd feel safer and have less self-doubt. You wouldn't be afraid to tell him how you feel."

"You didn't do that with Chris."

"I did so. I said I loved him first. And now we're engaged. You ought to try it." She sounded so happy.

"It wouldn't be that way with Blake. Believe me, I know."

"But you're in love with him. He sounds like such a great guy. Can't you give him more time?"

"I would if I thought it'd change things. Sex isn't enough for me. I need more. When Gran and Malcom exchanged vows, I realized I want to get married, too, to a man who's ready for that kind of commitment. There's no chance of that with Blake."

"Chris just got here, so I have to go. I'll leave you with one question. What if you're mistaken?"

* * *

FOR DAYS, Vi mulled over the conversation with Carmie. Could her friend be right? Was she wrong about Blake? He'd brought up the commitment thing weeks ago. Was it possible he might feel differently now or in the future?

She spent a few minutes before bed Sunday night standing tall and stating with heartfelt sincerity that she was pretty and worth any man's love. She did the same thing Monday and Tuesday mornings and evenings in front of the mirror, and again Wednesday before work. Once more in the privacy of her office before she left for the bike store to help celebrate the grand opening. Carmie had been right—talking to herself and meaning every word helped. She really did feel more confident. "What if I jumped to a conclusion about him that isn't true?" she asked her reflection.

There was only one way to find out. Talk to him about it. Tonight.

CHAPTER 28

From the minute Blake unlocked the doors of his new store Wednesday, he was swamped. The ads and radio spots had done their jobs. If not for Ross and Joanie helping with bike rentals, sales of cycling peripherals and bike orders from customers eager to buy, he'd have been in trouble.

As busy as he was, he kept an eye out for Vi. Knowing she'd be coming from work, he didn't expect to see her till late in the afternoon. He looked forward to celebrating with her and the team.

Earlier, Ross's girlfriend had stopped by. She seemed nice, and Ross was clearly crazy about her. Which amped up Blake's eagerness to see Vi.

By six o'clock, business had slowed down enough to relax. Blake ordered dinner for the three of them delivered from Hastings. Not long after they finished, a fresh crowd of biking enthusiasts showed up.

"I thought Vi was coming," Ross said when things quieted down again. "We close in less than an hour."

"She has that new job and is real busy," Blake explained. "She'll be here." But he was beginning to wonder. Something unexpected at DD Telecom might keep her from showing in time. "Let's straighten up in here."

They were hard at work when the door opened and Vi finally arrived.

Ross and Joanie greeted her with smiles. "You made it," Ross said. "You can finally stop checking the time every few minutes, Blake."

He gave a sheepish grin. He was awful glad to see her and relieved she'd made it. "Busy day?" he said, fighting to keep his hands off her.

"Pretty bad, but I survived. You got a haircut."

"Finally, right? Thought I should."

"Looks good." She glanced around. "The store looks really good. Those are beautiful flowers."

"They're from Grandpop and Caroline."

"So nice of them. Wish I'd thought of that."

"I didn't expect you to. Your being here is gift enough." He smiled into her eyes, but she didn't seem to notice. He sensed that once again, she'd pulled back. In the past, he'd put the blame on fatigue, but it'd happened enough that he was beginning to wonder what the real problem was.

"Was today as busy as you expected?" she asked.

"From the midday sales report, better. We'll find out more when we get the final tally after closing. I couldn't have made it through the day without these two," he said, jerking his thumb at his employees. "You guys are the best."

Joanie beamed. "I'm going to like working here. You're a darned good boss."

"What she said," Ross agreed.

Joanie glanced at the wall clock. "We close in twenty minutes. Mind if I print out the numbers now?"

Figuring they wouldn't see any more customers that night, Blake nodded. "Go ahead. You may as well get the deposit ready, too." He doubted they'd taken in much cash, as most customers paid with a card or by phone, but some had pulled out their wallets or written checks. "Why don't you restock the merchandise, Ross. If you're hungry, there are cookies left," he told Vi as his staff prepared to close for the day.

"I ate at my desk. Can I talk to you for a minute? In private."

Maybe she'd warm up again and congratulate him with a steamy kiss or three. Blake nodded. "Let's go into my office." He shut the door and started to reach for her.

Holding up both hands palms out, she stopped him. "Not now or I'll lose my nerve."

"Uh, what?"

"Just listen, okay?"

With her chin high and a fiery glint in her eyes, she was spectacular. Also somewhat intimidating. No telling what she'd say. He sucked in a breath and nodded for her to go ahead.

After murmuring something about self-confidence, she squared her shoulders. "We haven't known each other long, yet sometimes it feels like years. You're easy to talk to, and we laugh a lot."

He wanted to add that the sex was amazing, but kept quiet.

"Here's my question. Do we have a chance at a real relationship?"

"Aren't we in one of those now?"

"I mean a relationship with a future."

Talk about blindsiding him. His mind stumbled around, searching for an answer. She stared at him expectantly. "Where did that come from?" was all he came up with.

"Just answer the question."

At the moment, impossible. "I really like you, Vi. You know that."

"But?"

"I won't lie. It's too soon to commit."

"I'm aware of your feelings, but that's not what I'm asking about. I want to know if in the furthest stretch of your imagination you see a future for us."

Heck if he knew. Hadn't thought that far ahead. "This is a complete surprise. Can I let you know later?"

"Sure."

The way she said it and the dismissive flick of her hand prompted him to ask another question. "We'll still see each other in the meantime, right?"

"I don't think so, Blake."

Oh, man. "But you said...I thought...When did you decide this?"

"The day after the wedding. The vows Gran and Malcom exchanged and the obvious love between them really made me think. I want to be with a man interested in settling down and starting a family."

He couldn't have been more stunned if she'd sprouted a tree on her head. He realized his jaw was on the floor and shut his mouth.

"Call me when you've made up your mind."

"We can't see each other till then?" he repeated.

"I don't think so. Congratulations on the store opening. I'm glad it's a success."

She exited his office, said goodbye to Ross and Joanie, and left.

* * *

AFTER VI'S UNEXPECTED DEPARTURE, Blake's two employees stared at him with mixtures of sympathy and confusion. "You eavesdropped," he accused them.

"Didn't need to," Joanie said. "We heard it all."

Should've thought of soundproofing.

Ross shook his head. "By the look on your face, she crushed you."

"I'm in shock," Blake admitted. "She caught me totally by surprise."

"That was obvious. You blew it, man."

Blake scrubbed his hand over his face. "It just happened and hasn't sunk in yet, so lay off."

Joanie bit her lip. "I'm sorry, Blake. I think I know what Vi's talking about. Jack and I have been happily married for almost twelve years, but there was a time while we were dating when I got tired of us going along, getting along without any idea if he wanted a future with me. I asked him if we were ever going to get married. Like you, he didn't have an answer. We broke up for almost three months before he wised up."

Blake doubted Vi expected a proposal. It was way too soon for that, and they both knew it. Wanting to be alone, he shoved his hands in his pockets. "Give me the printout, Joanie, and go home. You, too, Ross. I'll make the deposit tonight. Thanks again, both of you."

Minutes later, they left. The numbers were thirty-two percent higher than he'd anticipated. Great news, but at the moment, he was too numb to care.

CHAPTER 29

Vi drove home both proud of herself for her show of self-confidence in front of Blake and also sick at heart. She'd been pretty sure he wouldn't want to commit, and she'd been right.

The tears started when she walked into the house and Mr. T ran to her and begged to be held. She picked him up and kissed his head. "I know you're like this because you want more food, but at least you love me for feeding you."

She texted Rose and Carmie. *I need you both. Please come over.*

Less than five minutes later, Rose let her know they were carpooling and on their way.

They came in together. One look at her face, and they led her to the couch and sat on either side of her. Comforting and supportive, and she appreciated them so much.

"What happened?" Rose asked and handed her a clean tissue from her purse.

"You two advised me to work on my self-confidence. I have been. Tonight, I screwed up my courage. I didn't mention commitment, simply asked Blake if he could possibly visualize a future together." Remembering, she broke into sobs. "He didn't have an answer, couldn't even think of one. In other words, he doesn't."

They consoled her with hugs and sympathetic murmurs. "You probably caught him off-guard, and he couldn't think," Rose said.

"That's right," Carmie agreed, "Tell me exactly what happened when you asked."

"He gaped at me and was speechless." Vi blew her nose. "As I suspected, his interest in me is mostly sexual."

Rose placed her hand on Vi's arm. "Could it be that he assumed sex was all you wanted?"

"I wouldn't know. We never talked about it." Vi exhaled a sad breath. "Or much else except to commiserate about Gran and Malcom. And a few other things, but very little about us."

"That's a conversation you might want to have with him later," Carmie advised. "Give him time to think and get back to you."

"What if he doesn't?" Vi's eyes filled again. "I'm thirty years old, my biological clock is ticking, and I want to get married and start a family. With or without him." Although the thought of dating and finding someone else seemed impossible.

Carmie's eyes widened. "When you make a decision, you don't waste any time."

"I've been thinking about marriage and kids for a while now. Tonight, I admitted it. And by the way, I've raised my standards. No more social misfits like the guys I've wasted so much time dating." She felt compelled to add, "If I hadn't met Blake, I wouldn't have realized the rut I stuck myself in to."

"Wow," Rose said. "You've come a long way."

"Exactly my thoughts," Carmie seconded. "In a way, your feelings for Blake helped solidify what you really want. I'm proud of you for speaking up, and I have faith that no matter what happens, you'll be all right."

"Thanks. I love you both, but it's getting late. You should go home."

When they left after a comforting group hug, Vi felt better.

* * *

TWO WEEKS PASSED without a word from Blake. As sad as Vi was, she refused to sit around moping. She poured herself into work and got together with her sister and Carmie and some of her friends at work. When Gran and Malcom returned from their honeymoon, she stopped by on Sunday to see them. They were both radiant and full of stories. Malcom had a doctor's appointment, a check-up on his rib. Claiming he was healed, he went anyway. Leaving Vi and Gran alone.

She told Gran about Blake without going into much detail. "We're not seeing each other right now, and I don't know if we will in the future," she finished, blinking back tears.

Gran laid a sympathetic hand over hers. "You really care about him, don't you? Malcom and I knew you belonged together that first night we all met at dinner."

Incredulous, Vi eyed her. "What?"

"That's why we talked you up."

"I don't remember that."

"I sang your praises and Malcom did the same with Blake."

"You deliberately tried to match us up?" Wait'll Blake heard about this. But she couldn't tell him because they weren't communicating anymore.

"That's right, and it worked."

"I wish. Blake isn't sure what he wants."

"I'm sorry, honey. Don't give up—he'll come to his senses."

Vi raised her chin. "If he doesn't, I'll move on," she vowed with a bravado she didn't feel.

"That's my girl," Gran said. "Keep me posted, all right?"

Vi nodded. Since the night she'd asked Blake about the future, her self-confidence had ebbed, but she remained determined to boost it up. She stood in front of the mirror every morning and every night assuring herself that she was attractive and worth a man's love. The more frequently she stated the words, the more she believed them.

"Eat your heart out, Blake," she said several times.

It helped.

CHAPTER 30

Saturday morning, Vi decided to take herself out for coffee and a doughnut at the Hastings where she and Carmie had met some weeks earlier. Of course, it was packed, and she placed her order to go. But the noise and bustle appealed to her more than being alone, and she decided to stay. All the tables were taken.

"There's a seat here," an attractive male about her age offered, gesturing at the lone empty chair in the room.

"Thanks," she said and sat.

They introduced themselves—his name was Max—and shared where they worked. A short time later, he opened up to her. "You might be able to help me out," he said, and launched into a long story about a fight with his girlfriend and his worries that she was cheating on him.

Wondering what she'd gotten herself into, Vi listened and sympathized.

"What should I do?" he said.

The whole thing was beyond her expertise. Not that she had much to begin with. She wanted to tell him about Blake and her own pain, but Max's situation was worse than hers. Besides, he needed to talk. She consoled him as best she could, even squeezed his forearm. "What you're going through is no fun," she said. "I wish I could help, but I don't have an answer. I do happen to know from experience that loving yourself goes a long way to feeling better. Good luck with whatever you decide."

"Thanks for listening. There's a guy on his way out looking at you."

She glanced toward the exit and saw Ross staring at her. She gave him a wan smile. He nodded and exited.

Strange. When she left a few minutes later, she forgot all about that.

* * *

As a rule, Blake took weekends off, but Grandpop had invited him to Saturday lunch, just the two of them. Figuring he wanted to talk about business and see printouts of recent sales, he headed for the new store to get copies. Ross and Joanie were working today, and he looked forward to seeing them. Anything to blunt the pain of life without Vi. He felt lost and missed her something awful, but refused to be pushed into a corner by her ultimatum.

Ross greeted him with surprise. "What are you doing here?"

"I came to pick up printouts of our recent numbers to share with my grandpa. Have we been busy this morning?"

"So far." Joanie left the room to print them out.

When she returned, Blake noted the somber look on Ross's face. "Why are you so serious? What's wrong?"

"You won't like this."

Blake hoped he wasn't going to give notice. He seemed happy here, but you never knew.

"I stopped for coffee earlier and saw Vi. She was with a guy."

Hadn't expected that. "Who was it?" he asked, gripping the pages of data.

"No idea, but he was good-looking."

Oh, man. Blake scrubbed his hand over his face. "Good to know. Gotta take off or I'll be late for lunch."

He met his grandfather in the dining room. "Where's Caroline?"

"Having lunch out with a few girlfriends. Sit down."

"I know you're interested in how the second store is doing. I brought a printout for the past two weeks."

"Forget that. What's with you and Vi?"

May as well tell him. "We're not seeing each other right now."

"And why is that?"

"She expects me to do what she wants."

"I can't read your mind, Blake. Spell it out."

"She wants a commitment about the future."

"Why the devil don't you give it to her?"

"Maybe I don't want to fall in love." Which was the truth.

Grandpop snorted. "You already have. You're scared, is that it?"

"I call it smart. I'm no fool. When a serious relationship ends, it hurts."

"Ah, it all comes clear. You lost your father and your mother pulled away from you. Two losses at once, terrible times." Grandpop narrowed his eyes. "Are you saying you'd rather be alone and protect your feelings than be with the woman who's crazy about you, makes you happy and could give you a lifetime of joy?" He shook his head. "You can be a real thick-headed idiot. Vi is the best thing to happen to you since I don't know when. If you're not careful, you'll lose her. Now, get out of here and do something about it."

CHAPTER 31

On the drive home, Blake thought about what his grandfather had said. On top of that, Ross had seen Vi with another guy.

Already testing out someone new? That really fried him.

He stewed about it for the rest of the day and into the night until James distracted him with a good news phone call. Whitney was in labor. Blake spent several hours at the hospital, staying until he welcomed his niece and nephew into the world. Tiny, funny-looking little humans who stared straight into his eyes with utter trust and melted his heart.

Instant love.

He slept a few hours, then woke up thinking about the babies, the miracle of birth and new life.

And understood that he wanted kids of his own.

With Vi.

As Grandpop had wisely pointed out, he loved her. Hadn't realized. He gave himself a mental smack in the head. How had he been so dense? His grandfather was right again—for a guy who was supposed to be smart, he was a real idiot.

Around dawn, he sent Vi a photo of James and Whitney each cradling a swaddled infant. *Meet Alexis and Emmett. Born at 1:22 this morning. I'm an uncle!*

He figured she'd be asleep, and her silence verified it. He'd brewed a pot of coffee, showered, dressed, and was contemplating breakfast when she replied.

So cute. Congrats to everyone!

That was it.

He'd expected more, wondered if she'd already moved on. Better go see her right away before it was too late. She didn't like when he dropped in unannounced, but if she didn't know he was on his way she couldn't tell him not to come.

He reached the complex in record time. At this early hour, the guest parking area was mostly empty. After he punched the doorbell several times, she finally answered. In her bathrobe.

"Blake. It's Sunday and barely eight a.m. What are you doing here so early?"

"When you texted back, I knew you were awake. You said to get in touch when I made up my mind, and here I am."

She gave him a wary look. "I suppose you want to come in."

"Please." He wiped his feet and stepped into the entry.

"There's coffee in the pot," she said and raked her hand through her hair. "I'll be back."

Despite the cup he'd already had at home, he needed another. After pouring himself a mug, he sat down at the eating counter.

Mr. T padded across the kitchen, let out a plaintive meow and butted his head against Blake's foot. Probably hungry. "I'm not sure where she went, but she'll feed you soon." He hopped off the bar stool and hunkered down to pet the cat. Loud purrs filled the air. "Like that, do you? You'd never guess I'm nervous, but I am." Busy enjoying the attention, Mr. T ignored the comment. "Easy for you to be your usual self. You're not about to change your life forever. Wish me luck."

Vi returned to the kitchen. She'd combed her hair and changed into jeans and a shirt. "Are you talking to Mr. T?"

"He's a good listener. I think he's hungry." Blake returned to the stool.

After feeding the animal, she refilled her mug and joined him at the eating bar. "Congrats on being an uncle. As soon as I got your text, I ordered a few gifts for the twins and their parents."

"Whitney will be pleased." He grinned. "Those babies are pretty special."

The conversation ended, the silence putting him on the spot. She wasn't making this easy. He cleared his throat. "How've you been?"

"Surviving, but I don't think that's why you're here. You said something about making up your mind?"

"Right. I've been doing a lot of thinking. The past few weeks without you have been rough. You're the only woman I want, Vi, and I don't want to lose you."

"I was beginning to wonder. It's been a few weeks since I heard from you."

He waited for her to say more, but she simply stared at him. Nothing like emotional guilt to make him confess. "Want a big shock? As it turns outs, I'm in love with you."

"You don't fall in love, remember? You start a relationship and things are good for a while. Then they aren't, and you move on."

Not the reaction he expected. "This is one of the many reasons why you fascinate me, Vi. You say unpredictable things that keep me on my toes." The furrows he'd grown used to and had missed appeared between her eyebrows, and he went on. "Like now. I figured you'd throw your arms around me and say you love me, too. Instead, you reminded me of something I said that isn't true anymore. When I originally said it, I was clueless about love. But you changed everything."

"Oh, really," she said as if she doubted that. "You thought you loved Sammi, then realized you'd confused love with lust. How do you know for sure you're not doing the same thing with me?"

This time, he didn't have to think about what to say. "For starters, the past few weeks without you drained my life of color. I hadn't understood how much you enriched everything. My feelings for you are different from anything in the past. I don't know how to describe it except there's a deep knowing in my chest and gut. Do I visualize a future with you? One hundred percent, a long and bright one. Without you beside me, everything is dull. To be honest though, I'm not ready to talk marriage yet. But I probably will be soon."

"Neither am I, although my biological clock is ticking and I don't want to wait too long. I agree that, yes, we do need more time together." She crossed her arms over her waist. "What *are* you ready for?"

"Uh-uh, it's your turn to answer my question," he countered. "Tell me about the man you had coffee with the other day."

"Where did you hear—Ross. When I saw him at Hastings, he gave me such a dark look."

"Who's this guy who asked you out?"

"You have it all wrong. The place was packed and he happened to have an empty chair at his table. He offered it to me."

"Did he hit on you?"

"No, and would it matter if he had? I wasn't interested. FYI, I'm in love with someone else."

Blake tipped up her chin. "Would that someone be me?"

She nodded. "You own my heart."

The tension roiling through his gut since she'd walked away faded. Not counting meeting the babies, he grinned for the first time in weeks. "I'll take good care of it. Come here, you."

"It's about time. I brushed my teeth and everything."

Chuckling, he pulled her into his arms. Then sobered, kissed her and held on tight. *Home.* "We have a lot to talk about, but first, I'm desperate to make love with you."

"Then follow me to the bedroom."

* * *

SOMETIME LATER, curled up beside Blake after fabulous sex, Vi was at last able to voice the words she'd once fought to silence. "I love you, Blake Wanamaker. You don't know how good it feels to say the words out loud to you."

"I get that. I love you, too," he said, smiling into her eyes.

"You don't understand. The last time we made love, I wanted to tell you, but I held back. I was afraid if you knew, you'd disappear so fast."

"If I had, I wouldn't have been able to stay away long."

"You couldn't have known that. Now I can think straight

265

again. You haven't said what you're ready for next in our relationship."

"For starters, I want us to be exclusive. You good with that?"

"Absolutely. Let's seal it with a kiss."

A long, sweet kiss later, he nuzzled her nose. "God above, I love you. Caroline and Grandpop will freak when we tell them."

"I doubt that. They've known from the start we'd end up together. Remember how they bragged to each other about us and embarrassed us at that first dinner? They did it because they wanted us to be impressed with each other and end up together. That's what Gran said."

Blake shook his head. "What a pair of schemers." He cocked an ear. "Is that your stomach I hear rumbling?"

"You have to ask?" she teased. "I'm running on empty. I'll bet you are, too."

"Let's shower and get dressed, then go out to breakfast."

Later, as they ate and laughed and discussed the future, everything fell into place and all was right with the world.

The End

ALSO BY ANN ROTH

Port Simms

Who's Getting Married

Ann Roth Classics

A Place to Belong

Father of the Year

Another Life

My Sisters

Dunlin Shores

Book 1 Just the Way You Are

Book 2 Wedding Bell Blues

Book 3 Falling for Mr. Wrong

Book 4: A Special Kind of Love

Heroes of Rogue Valley

Book 1 Mr. January

Book 2 Mr. February

Book 3 Mr. March

Book 4: Mr. April

Book 5: Mr. May

Book 6: Mr. June

Book 7: Mr. July

Book 8: Mr. August

Book 9: Mr. September

Book 10: Mr. December

Halo Island

Book 1 All I Want for Christmas

Book 2 The Pilot's Woman

Book 3 Ooh, Baby!

Book 4 The One I Love

Miracle Falls

Book 1 Christmas in Miracle Falls

Book 2 Dream a Little Dream

Book 3 It Had to Be You

Book 4: You're the One That I Want

Book 5 There's Something About You

Book 6 My Heart Belongs to You

Saddlers Prairie

Book 1 Since I Fell for You

Book 2 I'll Be There

Book 3 Until There Was You

Book 4 Got My Heart Set On You

ABOUT THE AUTHOR

Ann Roth is an award-winning author of 40-plus contemporary romance and women's fiction novels, as well as novellas and numerous short stories. Her first novel was published in 2000 by Harlequin Special Edition and was nominated by *Romantic Times* as best first book. Ann lives with the love of her life in the Greater Seattle area and enjoys creating flawed characters and putting them in challenging situations that help them grow and ultimately find love— whether or not they're looking for it.

Find out about new releases!
Sign up for my newsletter